W9-BEZ-809

Scenes from the Homefront

Scenes from the Homefront

SARA VOGAN

BANTAM BOOKS
NEW YORK · TORONTO · LONDON · SYDNEY · AUCKLAND

*Publication of this work was supported in part
by grants from the Illinois Arts Council, a state agency,
and the National Endowment for the Arts.*

*This edition contains the complete text
of the original hardcover edition.*
NOT ONE WORD HAS BEEN OMITTED.

SCENES FROM THE HOMEFRONT
A Bantam Book / published by arrangement with University of Illinois Press

PRINTING HISTORY
University of Illinois Press edition published 1987

"Scenes from the Homefront," Antaeus, *Autumn 1979;* Pushcart Prize V, *1980;* Quarto, *Number 24, December 1981 (British).*
"No Other Women," Intro 9, *1978;* The Best of Intro, *1985.*
"Miss Buick of 1942," Quarterly West, *Winter 1978; Distinguished Stories,* Best American Short Stories, *1979; Outstanding Writers,* Pushcart Prize IV, *1979.*
"Angels in the Snow," Canard Anthology, *1983.*
"The Confession of the Finch," Cream City Review, *Volume 7, Number 2, 1982.*
"The Strength of Steel," ZYZZYVA, *Volume 2, Number 1, 1986.*
"Sunday's No Name Band," The Available Press/PEN Short Stories, *1985;* The Graywolf Annual Two, *Stories by Women, 1986.*
"China across the Bay," Willow Springs, *Number 7, Fall 1980; Outstanding Writers,* Pushcart Prize VI, *1981–1982.*
"Mozart in the Afternoon," Cutbank 6, *Spring 1976; Distinguished Stories,* Best American Short Stories, *1977.*
"Hearts of a Shark," Carolina Quarterly, *Fall 1976.*

Bantam edition / October 1989

*All rights reserved.
Copyright © 1987 by Sara Vogan.
Cover art copyright © 1989 by Gary Kelley.
No part of this book may be reproduced or transmitted in any form or by any means, electronic or mechanical,
including photocopying, recording, or by any information storage and retrieval system, without permission in
writing from the publisher.
For information address: University of Illinois Press,
54 E. Gregory Drive, Champaign, IL 61820.*

Library of Congress Cataloging-in-Publication Data

Vogan, Sara.
   Scenes from the homefront / Sara Vogan.
      p.   cm.
   Contents: Scenes from the homefront — No other women — Miss Buick of
1942 — The crane wife — Angels in the snow — The confession of the
finch — The strength of steel — Sunday's no name band — China across the
bay — Mozart in the afternoon — Hearts of a shark.
   ISBN 0-553-34751-9
   I. Title.
PS3572.029S34   1989   89-6972
813'.54—dc20   CIP

Published simultaneously in the United States and Canada

*Bantam Books are published by Bantam Books, a division of Bantam
Doubleday Dell Publishing Group, Inc. Its trademark, consisting of the
words "Bantam Books" and the portrayal of a rooster, is Registered in
U.S. Patent and Trademark Office and in other countries. Marca Regis-
trada. Bantam Books, 666 Fifth Avenue, New York, New York 10103.*

PRINTED IN THE UNITED STATES OF AMERICA

O   0 9 8 7 6 5 4 3 2 1

For my parents, Bette and Jim

with special thanks
to David and Brenda

Contents

Scenes from the Homefront

Scenes from the Homefront

On the day my father was born Kaiser Wilhelm II was planning the invasion of Belgium although he would not declare war for another six weeks. In Shenandoah, Pennsylvania, coal dust drifted through the cracks in the windows where my grandmother, a girl of seventeen, was in labor. My grandfather, fifty years old and probably wearing his usual white suit, paced in the living room and awaited the birth of his first child.

It was a breech birth and, as was common at the time, the doctor had to break both my father's arms during delivery. The baby was healthy except for the muscles of his right eye. Many children are born like my father, with tight muscles in their eyes. Doctors still cut those muscles so they will grow back the proper length and the eye will look forward, not inward to the side of the nose as my father's did. But the doctor who delivered my father cut a little too deep. He snipped the optic nerve and blinded my father permanently in his right eye.

My grandfather was too old to serve in World War I. By the time his first child was ten, my grandfather was senile. He lived to be ninety-three, seeing World War I, the Spanish civil war, World War II, and the Korean Conflict. But in the last part of his life my grandfather lived mostly in the Civil War. He had been named Ulysses Simpson Grant Vogan, presumably after the general and president, who was perhaps a relative, although we never knew for sure. U. G., or Grant as my mother called him, seemed to have Southern sympathies. From the middle 1920s until he died in 1957, Ulysses Simpson Grant Vogan believed himself to be Robert E. Lee and sometimes Clarence Darrow. By the time I knew him no one bothered to correct him anymore. He told me about the Monkey Trial and John Scopes. He told me about his surrender at Appomattox. Talking about the Monkey Trial made him sweat and swear and smile. "Never charged that fellow a penny," he always said. "You can't buy the truth." When he talked about Appomattox he sometimes wet himself, the yellow stain creeping down the front of his white linen suit.

My grandfather believed his daughter, Annie, died in North Carolina in 1862 after the Second Bull Run. "I was a soldier then," he always said. "I couldn't let the men see my tears."

One night as my mother tucked me into bed she said, "You can't believe everything Grant tells you. He's confused a lot of the time."

"Because he was a soldier?"

"No. Not that." She fussed with my blankets. "Your Aunt Ann died back in the twenties. From mumps."

"How do you know?" At that age anything was possible, like the swelling of my mother before my baby brother was born.

"Your father told me. Now go to sleep."

I thought she had violated some grown-up law that had to do with what parents couldn't say "in front of the children." Listening at night to the whispered sounds from their bedroom next door, I assumed they told stories they couldn't tell

me. My father never spoke of Ann, but then he seldom talked about his family, not even about his younger brother Robert. All I knew then about my Uncle Robert was that he joined the U.S. Army in 1941 at the beginning of American involvement in World War II.

My father could not join the service; not one branch would take him because of his bad eye. He looked perfectly normal, both of his hazel eyes seeming to draw in all the light from the room. But with his vision limited to only one eye he had no peripheral vision and no depth perception. I always imagined he must see the world flattened out like an Egyptian hieroglyphic or perhaps the way Mondrian might have painted a landscape.

If my father could not fight he would not sit behind a desk and record the fighting of others. When he met my mother in 1943 he was in private business, repossessing used cars.

They did not have a family right away. "It wouldn't have seemed right, with the war on," my father told me once. But when the war was won my father decided the time was right and I was born shortly thereafter. I should have been a boy; the birth certificate was all filled out, an act of my father's as he paced in the hospital waiting room. They renamed me after my mother.

My Uncle Robert had married a Canadian woman he met in Trenton before he shipped out for the European theater. Uncle Robert's last letter came in 1942, congratulating his wife on the birth of their boy. She received no letters from him after that, nor did my father or his parents. The Army investigation could only report he picked up his last pay parcel in October 1942. There was no more news of him, no confirmation he had died or deserted, no record of his capture. I remember his homecoming in 1953. I don't know where he had been all those years and neither does my father. I imagine Robert became a spy, or perhaps took a lover and lived in Paris. I wonder what his wife, my aunt, felt during all those years. I wonder if she knew he would come back to her.

On a June morning in 1953 Robert walked into the living room of his wife's house in Trenton. He was wearing his Army uniform. "I bet you don't know who I am," he said to my cousin, ten at the time. "I'm your father. Is your mother at home?"

They came to see us, Uncle Robert still wearing his Army uniform but without any medals, no color on the drab green except for the yellow U.S. Army insignia on his shoulder.

I didn't know him and had heard almost nothing about him. But I knew what to say. "Where were you?" I asked, parroting the questions of my parents. He sat me on his lap and ran his hand over my head, down my back. He stroked my legs.

"All over," he said. "Do you know Vogan is a Prussian name?"

I shook my head.

"The only good thing about being Prussian is that Prussia doesn't exist anymore," he said.

I nodded solemnly, not sure I understood what he was telling me.

"Remember that when you get married," he said. "Don't marry a man with a German name."

"Why?"

"And don't marry any foreigners. In China and Japan they use the same word for woman and dustpan."

My grandfather was angry when he saw my uncle. His voice was measured. "I'm glad you're safe," he said. "But the men are all lost. All of them trapped. Damn minié balls!" My grandfather shook his head sadly. "Did you get the message through? Are the reinforcements coming?"

They left abruptly one morning and I never saw my Uncle Robert or his family again. Later I was told they moved away. Robert and my father had quarreled, about my grandfather, I suppose. About the war, maybe. We never saw them after that and received no cards at Christmas.

The war was important to my father. For him it never ended. Each year we planted a victory garden. My mother, my brother, and I would hoe, sow seeds, pull weeds, and build scarecrows. My mother canned and made me help her while my brother picked and washed the fresh vegetables. In the late fifties we stopped eating the home-canned beans and peas. Instead my father made us store them in the basement along with fifty-five-gallon drums of distilled water. We had the first fallout shelter on our block. My brother and I wanted a swimming pool.

In his pine-paneled den my father kept a memorial to the war, a wall full of books on the campaigns, biographies of the generals, memoirs of the survivors. There was a closet full of magazines from the forties, dog-eared and yellowed with age. When my father tucked my brother and me in for the night he would bring along an old *Life* or *Saturday Evening Post,* sometimes *Colliers.* Often he keyed the magazines to the day. "On this very day, eleven years ago the Allied Forces . . ." We would sit on the bed and look at pictures of the dead, the pyrotechnics of bursting bombs and burning ships. He showed us pictures of Africa and the Aleutians, of gutted towns in Sicily and Japan. He made us identify airplanes and ships by letter and number. My brother loved the machines, the Green Dragons, Alligator Tanks, Amphibious Ducks. "You can't understand peace if you don't realize the nature of war," my father would say, "All these people will have died in vain if you won't look at them."

He helped us with our homework. Math and spelling were his favorite subjects. My brother, three years younger than I, worked the same problems I did, tutored by my father through a year of sixth-grade math when my brother was only in the third grade.

"Okay," my father would say. "If a tank is traveling at thirty miles an hour along a well-defended road toward a beach and a cargo carrier is offshore sailing along at forty-two miles an hour, first, let's figure how fast the ship is going in knots. That's how they measure a ship's speed, in knots."

"But what about the two trains going to Chicago?" I would ask.

"It's the same. See, one train at thirty, one train at forty-two. I'm just making it more interesting."

"You are not," I would say. "You're just making it harder."

My father would laugh. "I bet your brother can do it, can't you, Doug?" And my brother would smile because he knew my father would help him if he only looked puzzled and tried.

"Let's do spelling," my father would say. I handed him my list and went to stand in line next to my brother. "Campaign," my father would say.

"That's not on the list. The first word is sincerely."

"Is it going to hurt you to learn to spell campaign?"

"It won't do any good. I have to learn to spell sincerely."

"I bet Doug can do it. Want to try campaign? It's a C word, not a K."

We had a swing set behind the garden. Kicking my legs harder and harder, I pushed the swing in its half-arc above the rows of tomato plants, the long green leaves of the onions. The tomatoes became trees, the onions hedgerows, and if I squinted my eyes I could make the neat rows my mother set out go askew and a small village would form. Sometimes I would place rocks in the garden and swing as fast as I could. The rocks became houses. I was flying.

"I'm Sky King!" I would yell, pumping with my legs as the rusted swing chains screamed. "I'm flying!"

My brother threw a rock at me. It hit me on the foot. "You are not," he said. "I'm Sky King."

I wobbled down from my flying arc, the swing swaying back and forth, up and down, losing momentum. "I am too Sky King," I said. "I can go higher than you."

"You're just a girl. You have to be Penny."

"I'll beat you up." I began to limp across the yard toward my brother, who retreated, throwing rocks.

"I'll tell Dad."

"I'll break your mouth so you can't talk." I heaved a rock from my village at him.

"I'm Sky King!" he hollered, running away from me now. "I'm the Red Baron! Lucky Lindy!"

I could hear my brother laugh as he disappeared around the corner. "You," he called, hidden by the house. "Florence Nightingale. Betsy Ross. I Love Lucy." He took off running up the road. "And they can't fly!"

I was crying because my foot hurt and knelt to see where the bruise would form. Behind me the swing hung motionless in the hot air. I could get right back on. I could put the rocks back in my village, hop on my swing, and fly bombing missions over Germany, Japan. Instead I pulled out all my mother's tomato plants, crying as I cut down the trees in my village.

·   ·   ·

In school we studied world history every three years, and I don't remember getting past the invasion of Poland. The next year we would start again with American history and finish the Civil War by Christmas. My grandfather would complain. He once burned my *American History for Junior Scholars*, saying it was a piece of "Yankee propaganda crap." He took it to his room and burned each offending page separately with a match over the wastebasket, no one paying any attention to him until he asked my mother for a third pack of matches.

"They never get it right," he said. "They never tell our side."

Spring semester took us through World War I, and we generally got to the Great Depression, but it would be time for summer vacation before we could start the New Deal. The next fall would be a Current Events year and we would begin with the Cold War. I once figured if we went to school year round like children in Europe we would be at Pearl Harbor on the Fourth of July.

My father filled our summers with facts from World War II. Unlike other children our age, my brother and I learned early never to say "There's nothing to do." Out would come the magazines, the hardbound books, and we would sit in the den and read or stare at the pictures. I looked at the dead men in my father's collection, their twisted arms and mud-covered faces. Men die with their mouths open; some look like they are smiling. Only the living men look somber, their eyes growing larger as the war goes on. The men in the German camps are nothing but eyes, dark rags for clothes, mouths clamped shut, then the eyes, like matching bullet holes in their heads.

"The only suitable occupation for a gentleman is a soldier," my grandfather would say. "In times of peace he fights for freedom with his mind, not his arms." Shortly before he died my grandfather's two fantasies became integrated. He believed that as a young man he had run his wife's plantation at Arlington in Virginia, treating their Negroes kindly because Negroes could not take care of themselves. After his surrender at Appomattox he took up law again and practiced the Scopes case year after year. "You fight for the truth," he always said. "That young Scopes, he knows. Faith in the truth, that's the ticket."

He wanted to die a soldier and be buried beneath his Confederate flag. Sometimes he searched the house, trying to remember where he had mislaid it. Other days he remembered giving it to Grant at the Surrender and would walk into town saying "Steady, Traveller." Somewhere in the heart of our city my grandfather believed there was a flagmaker who would make him a new flag and blow holes in it to simulate one taken from the field. "The men won't mind," he always said. "So much was lost during the War."

When my grandfather died in 1957 Uncle Robert and his family sent a horseshoe wreath that would have looked better draped over the sweating neck of a Derby winner. There was no card.

"When you were little," I asked my mother, "what did you want to be?" She was washing dishes and I was drying. Even at that age I knew dish drying for what it actually was—a waste of time. The dishes would dry in the rack without my help. But I dried them for her anyway. It was what we did after dinner.

"I wanted to marry your father," she said.

"Did you know him then?"

"Oh no. Not until much later."

"How did you know it was him?"

My mother smiled at me. "You don't need to know all this now." She stuck her hands back in the dishwater.

I persisted. "But didn't you want to be anything just for yourself?"

"Oh I guess." She placed another dish in the rack. "For a long time I wanted to be like Eleanor Roosevelt. I always saw her as the power behind the throne."

I picked up a dish and dried it, thinking of Eleanor Roosevelt. My images of the president's wife must have been much different from my mother's. Mrs. Roosevelt looked like my grandmother, gone big in the bones so her weight seemed to rest in her hips and shoulders, not on the balls of her feet the way my mother's did. The face was pouchy, which I assumed happened because F. D. R. had died. That was what happened to women when their husbands died. It had happened to my grandmother. It would happen to my mother. Perhaps it came from too much crying.

In my father's magazines there was one picture of Eleanor Roosevelt with her hands folded in her lap. The fingers seemed blunted, and ropes of veins curled up her arms. She wasn't smiling. I didn't believe my mother wanted to be like Eleanor Roosevelt.

"Didn't you want to be anything else?"

She put another dish in the rack. "Before I met your father I thought a lot about Amelia Earhart. During the War I wanted to join the Air Force. WAFs. But it would have hurt your father's feelings." She turned and dried her hands on my towel. "And then I would have missed you." She smiled as if that sealed it.

For my twelfth birthday my father bought me a book of photographs by Margaret Bourke-White. I expected to see all the old famous pictures, the ones that were repeated in different magazines. London schoolchildren huddled in a ditch staring with large eyes at the planes fighting overhead. Hitler mounting the steps flanked by his storm troopers and a corridor of swastikas. The blind Australian in Buna helped down the road by an aborigine. But these were new pictures. We sat on the couch and looked at them together, leafing over the text my father told me I should read later. These were all pictures of Russians. Women holding rakes over their shoulders. Women in kerchiefs kneeling in church. The lighted paths of the bombs falling on the Kremlin at night. Joseph Stalin with a cigarette in his hand.

"A very important lady," my father said. "Her pictures made people see."

That year for Christmas I got a camera I wasn't allowed to touch because I was too young. My father would set the exposure, focus the lens, and stand behind me as I released the shutter. "You can be like Margaret Bourke-White when you grow up," my father said. "She took pictures of a lot of important things. Battles. Bomb sites. The way the women worked for the war." He set all the dials and lenses on the camera and placed it in my hands. "You have to have steady hands for a job like this," he said as he settled himself into his favorite chair, posing for his photograph. "And chemistry. Be sure to take chemistry in school." He smiled. "Okay. Shoot. Cheese."

In school we learned that swastika originally meant good luck in light, life, and love, a combination of the four L's. Swastikas have been found in excavations of ancient Rome, on Chinese coins, and in the sites of the Mound Builders in Mexico. We learned American Indians believed photographs would steal their souls.

*   *   *

"Don't marry a small man," my father said. "They have problems you can never imagine." Only tall boys were allowed to take me to basketball games and high-school dances. Although only of medium height himself, my father had evolved some theory about personality and height. "Hitler was a small man," he always said. "A small country too. Germany isn't as big as Pennsylvania. Tojo and Japan. Look at Japan." He told me small men and countries start wars to prove they are big enough to be bullies. He explained the guns-and-butter theory of economics. Germany needed copper and coal. "And Japan. Lord knows what they thought they needed." Over the years my father decided it was merely prestige the Japanese wanted, with China, such a big country, lying over their shoulders across the Sea of Japan.

"Look at Ike and MacArthur, at least six feet, each of them." And then he gave me the heights of the enemy personnel. Club-footed Goebbels was only five foot two.

Over iced drinks in the dark of a summer evening, the fireflies and our cigarettes the only light against a cloudy sky, my father and I talked about History. History with a capital H, just as he always said War with a capital W. The History of the War 1939–45. I was careful not to mention him at all. My father had aged, but perhaps that evening was the first time I noticed. In the last few years I had looked only at my own body, worrying about the fat on my hips, the budding of my breasts, or I had been watching others looking at my body, analyzing it, fantasizing about it. But in the dying light of the evening I could see the sag of his profile, the softness of his chin, the weight under his eyes. I asked him about the War. Not my war, but his war.

"I used to think it was Hitler's fault," he said. "But then my Dad thought the Civil War was started by Harriet Beecher

Stowe." He rattled the ice in his glass and I knew if I didn't say something the moment would pass and he would rise, ask me if I would like another drink, and retreat into the house. When he returned we would talk of different things, the new car he had his eye on, his plans for retirement.

"Was it the same?" I asked. "The same as this one?"

His cigarette glowed. Fathers have a way of being fathers forever. Their children, though grown with lives of their own, are always children to their fathers. It was a child's question, the timing too slow, the voice too timid.

"I was a young man then," he said. "Things seem very important to young men. We believed we were fighting the last war. The War to End All Wars. Of course," he laughed, "we were wrong. Maybe all young men are wrong."

"Why aren't you against this war?" the child again.

He said, "The problem with you peaceniks is that you're too young to understand love. The kind of love that causes wars, or at any rate keeps them going. Love of our country, our way of life. The Germans were fighting for that too."

I didn't understand then, maybe not now. "Where's the love in blowing babies to bits? Bombing rice paddies and bamboo huts?"

"The love is here," he said as he tapped his chest. "And here." He swept his arm across the darkening yard. "I'll tell you something corny, then maybe you'll understand. When I was trying to join the service I was looking for this mental picture. All those months from office to office I kept my eyes open for a picture I could take with me overseas. And one day I saw it. I concentrated on it so it would be mine. I can still see it.

"It's a girl, a young woman. It's summer and she's wearing a limegreen dress and white shoes. Her hair is blonde and curly, down to her shoulders. Soft. And she stands under a cottonwood tree, patterned by the shade. There's a creek and she's casting crumbs to some ducks. Behind her, up the hill, is a white farmhouse."

He was quiet for a moment. "I'd go for that. I'd fight for that. I'd burn babies, as you say. Drop bombs. For you. For your mother. But maybe you have to be older to understand why."

"I don't think age will change my mind about this war," I said, and I felt guilty as if I had deliberately misunderstood.

He shifted in his chair, cleared his throat. "Do you know the mystery writer Dashiell Hammett? You're a bright college girl, you ought to know about him."

"What's that got to do with anything?" He wasn't going to let me grow up; I would be trapped in his summer-green photograph forever.

"He was an interesting fellow. Had TB. Signed up for the war anyhow. Served in the Aleutians. And when McCarthy was on his tail he still wanted to fight. Even with a lot of the country against him. It's that kind of love."

He rose, rattling his glass loudly, and I silently held out mine. "I'd have gone," he said as he moved toward the door. "If they had let me."

In college I took photography and forged student identification cards. They were easy, the hard part was stealing the special paper from the university supply house. We would make up names and Social Security numbers, and I took mug shots of men I would claim to have married. We bought a damaged carton of marriage certificates at a fire sale and two gold-plated wedding bands.

The rides to the border were at night, the three of us, the guide, myself the bride, and the boy, all sitting in the front seat staring at the road revealed through the yellow headlights. Our talk was quiet; we were part of the resistance and felt this was something important and dangerous. Our guide seldom spoke after he gave us the instructions and any piece of news we might need.

I took the ride nine times and now some of the boys seem to run together. One cried and asked if I would hold him, and I did, feeling no warmth or excitement, only his pain and fear. A few years ago I heard that one committed suicide in Sweden, but I couldn't remember his face. Just last year one of the boys, a man now with a wife and child, stopped me in a shopping mall in Ohio.

We left the guide at our safe house, put New York license plates on the car. The boy and I checked into a motel, a different one each time.

In the morning, the boy and I would pretend to be newlyweds and would wander hand in hand through the sights on the American side of Niagara Falls. We would look in expensive souvenir shops, eat lunch in fancy restaurants, kiss each other in public, especially in front of policemen. We would lean over the guard rails and look into the foaming gorge. At three o'clock I would look at my husband for the day and tell him it was time. Some of them laughed. All of them wanted to delay it, to get drunk or stoned, to go over the bridge under the cover of darkness.

With a throng of tourists, we went over to Canada, presenting our forged identification papers to the border guards and assuring them we were only sightseers visiting for the day. We were never stopped. I've been told we were lucky; other couples had tried it and failed.

We looked at the Floral Clock, more gift shops, gave a last backward glance at the falls before making our way to a side street and a small quiet bar where all the signs were printed in French and English. Two men would be sitting at a table in the back playing dominoes. We would join them, have a drink, swap rings and the extra IDs. None of the boys changed their minds, but one got very drunk before the Canadian could lead him out of the bar. One boy kissed me, thanking me for my help. They each left, some to Toronto, some as far away as Winnipeg or Halifax. My husband for the day would begin his new life, his new identity, as a deserter from the Vietnam War.

The other domino player would go back across the border with me. Sometimes we would kiss. We always came back after dark.

In 1968 my father flew to Oklahoma for Uncle Robert's funeral. When he returned a week later my father told us his brother had committed suicide. With tears in his eyes my father said Robert gassed himself in a sealed room. Then he began to sob in my mother's arms, his tears rolling down her neck and making pale spots on the shoulders of her blouse. My brother left the room, motioning for me to follow. But I stayed, watching my father cry and the way my mother rocked him in her arms.

Later, when he had more control, my father told us we had four new cousins, mostly grown now, the sons and daughters of my Uncle Robert who were born after his return from the War. My eldest cousin has two children of his own, boys. My eldest cousin is a lieutenant in the Air Force.

My father wasn't political except when it came to Eisenhower. In my father's mind the General could make no mistakes and his presidency was perfect. Ike was his man and Richard Nixon was his second favorite. "Democrats start wars," he always said. "They leave it to the Republicans to finish them." He would laugh then. "And we have never lost a war."

In high school my brother was a wrestler, tall and very thin. My father thought he should play basketball but approved of wrestling when he decided the West Point basketball team was of not much account. My brother could go to West Point when he graduated, or to the Air Force Academy if he wished. My brother didn't even apply to West Point and lied to my father about the forms he never filled out. With the memory of the pictures in the worn magazines, and with the TV news covering the Vietnam War every evening, my brother decided he wanted to be a television cameraman and go to the journalism school at Northwestern. My brother's lottery number was thirteen—very high on the scale—and my father was pleased. "This time thirteen is a lucky number," my father told his friends.

My brother was six foot four and wrestled in the 180 class. Most wrestlers in that class are brawny, but my brother was wiry and quick. His metabolism was like mercury, adjustable to any change. The U.S. Army will take a six-foot-four male if he is over 140 pounds and under 248. For his first Army physical my brother weighed in at 136.

"Jesus Christ God Damn It!" my father shouted, pounding his fist on the table when he heard the news.

My brother laughed at him. "You know, I was nine years old before I realized that wasn't my real name. Jesus Christ God Damn It."

"A goddamned subversive, that's what you are."

My mother and I picked carefully at our food. I could tell by the look on her face, set tight and unblinking, that she would let them fight. She had defended my brother when he didn't go to West Point, soothed my father's disappointment, covered my brother's lies. But she would be quiet tonight.

My brother looked across the dinner table and over my shoulder. Walter Cronkite was reporting the number of Vietnamese dead for that day. "I don't want to fight," he said.

"And why the hell not?"

"This war is a mistake."

"A mistake? Says who? You? You know so goddamned much you can decide this country's foreign policy? You don't even have to shave every day."

My brother was calm, listing his answers as if this were a test. "I know we're overextended. I know it's none of our business. I know people on both sides are dying for nothing."

"It is your duty," my father said, making the words sound as if they were in capital, three-dimensional letters. "It is as inevitable as the fact your sister will have children. Able-bodied men have a moral duty to defend their country."

"No one is attacking us. We are doing the attacking."

My father took a deep, shaky breath. His eyes were black pits, rimmed with the red of his shame and frustration. "You are a coward. I have raised a coward."

"I'm not going," my brother said again. "If this weight thing doesn't work I'll go to Canada."

"You are not my son," my father said. "You are a coward piece of trash. A no-talent, lying cheat. A dog has more loyalty than you."

"What do you want from me? My body in a pine box? Dog tags hanging over the mantel?"

"Yes!" my father shouted, rising from the table. "I want a son I can be proud of."

"All you want is another number on the TV news. Do you think anyone is going to notice if Douglas MacArthur Vogan is killed in action? Name any of the dead ones, American, Vietnamese. One soldier on either side you can name and remember." My brother rose slowly and pushed back his chair as if squaring off for a fight. "I don't believe this is even happening. The bodies don't look human. Melted flesh. Pairs of ears strung on wires. It's a TV movie. They march the recruits into the ovens just like at Dachau. Vietnam doesn't exist."

I could see the lie of that statement in my brother's face. After school and in the summers my brother worked at a small manufacturing company, Hannah's Orthopedic Devices, where they made prostheses. Mr. Hannah, who used to play checkers with my grandfather, was expanding. The war brought new orders from the VA hospital for feet, legs, arms, mechanical hands. My brother delivered them, brought them back if they didn't fit.

My father sat down again, leaving my brother standing alone in the room above the rest of us. I watched my brother staring down at my father, his eyes sunk deep in his face, the bones just visible beneath the skin.

"That's your trouble," my father said. "You have no faith. Faith is everything. Even the Germans and Japanese believed in their countries."

"The Germans believed in gassing Jews. Some faith."

"In the long run maybe what those men did was wrong. But you have to grant a certain admiration to those kamikaze pilots. They kissed their wives and children good-bye and flew their planes out over the ocean. An amazing act of faith."

I looked at my mother, who was still studying her food. "It's not the same," I said.

"You stay out of this," my father said. My mother put her hand on my arm. "Women and children don't fight," he said. "This is none of your business."

"He's my brother."

"Cool it," my brother told me. "I'm not going to Nam. I'll fight here."

"You just don't understand," my father said, his voice almost pleading this time.

My brother looked him dead in the eye.

"No," my father said. "You fight this war for the good of your country. It's what makes us what we are today."

"Terrific," my brother said. "You want me to fight for a

country that's made it possible to blow up the entire world. It's like Hitler recruiting Jew-gassers."

"You were born in a hospital," my father said with tears in his eyes. "You are strong and healthy. When I was a kid children still died of mumps. Polio. You fight for science. Your health. Your education. The freedom you have to make this decision to abandon the principles that made you what you are. If you won't defend those ideals you are no son of mine."

"You want me to go because you couldn't."

My father rose to leave the table. "Children are only the dreams of their parents."

Just recently my father retired and took my mother on a trip around the world. They visited battlefields. I can see my father standing by the sea, his arm sweeping across the horizon as he points out to my mother where the ships must have moored, how the landing craft pulled up to Omaha Beach as the Germans fired from the safety of their bunkers. Behind them stand acres of white crosses, the names of the dead facing the sea. My parents stand beside a concrete sphere, remnant of the Maginot Line that was supposed to defend France. They walk through Dachau to stare at the showers, pick through the rubble of Cassino to see the stones of the monastery.

They send postcards to me and my brother, brightly colored pictures in contrast to the severe photographs from our childhood. My brother laughed when I talked to him on the phone. "When I was a kid I thought America was the only country in color. The rest of the world was in black and white," he said.

We get postcards of smiling Dutch girls, children playing in a fountain in Rome. Europe disappointed my father. Most of the scars were hidden, he said. "Europe is a lie," he wrote on the back of a card from Ardennes. "Historical battles that changed the course of the world have been fought here. Europeans try to hide that. No one will talk about The War. A French wine merchant said to me: 'Which one? There were so many.'"

My mother loved Hawaii; my father hated Pearl Harbor. He sent me a postcard of the burning of the USS *West Virginia*, small boats in the foreground spraying water across her decks, the flag of the USS *Arizona* waving in the background. "Some of them have forgotten," the card said. In my mother's hand across the bottom was a postscript: "It has rained the whole time we have been here."

My father loved the Pacific Theater. The climate might have hidden the scars there, but at least the people hadn't. In New Guinea my father said you could look out over a field in a tropical forest and it would look as even as the back of your hand. But walking through it you went up and down through bomb craters, the plants in the depressions growing taller than the rest to give the appearance of evenness. They toured the tinier islands, my father explaining to my mother their strategic importance. He recounted for her the Battle of Boat 13, unlucky enough to have landed its troops in front of a Japanese pillbox. My mother knows the story, as do I. My father had read it to us out of an old *Life* magazine, a February issue saved from 1944.

Flying across the Pacific, my father wants to see buoys or plaques marking the surface of the ocean like white crosses placed beside roads. He wants billboards erected on the sea. "The USS *Wasp* was torpedoed here by a Japanese submarine while sailing in convoy to Guadalcanal. Ninety-two percent of her crew were lost although twenty-three Americans floated in a rubber raft for eighteen days before being picked up off Port Moresby."

They were denied permission to go into Vietnam, but

my father didn't seem disappointed. "It wouldn't be safe for your mother," he wrote. "It probably looks just like the rest."

A few years before my grandfather died we took him to Gettysburg as part of our vacation. My father thought my brother and I should have a normal view of the Civil War, a view not colored by his father's fantasies. In the car my mother wanted me to play a card game with my brother, but I refused for no reason I could explain then. My attention was on my grandfather, the look on his face as he watched the countryside rolling by. We had to stop once because my grandfather wet himself and the smell of his urine threatened to make my brother sick. My grandfather said nothing during the drive, and I watched his face, unable to read anything into his ninety-year-old features.

We stood on the battlefield and read the signs, listened to the guides, and picked up handfuls of brochures. We saw where the Union soldiers built their reinforcements, the trenches now mortared together with cement to keep tourists from stealing the field stones. Guides with loudspeakers walked little groups of us around the site of the three-day battle, describing what happened at each spot.

My grandfather began to cry. We walked him over to the shade of a tree, away from the guide and the sound of his loudspeaker. "All those lives," he said through his tears, and my mother offered him her handkerchief. "Thousands of men, just farmers. Lost. All lost." He cried as he told us the story of his most bitter defeat, and my mother sat with her hand on his shoulder while my father turned his back and walked away.

"They had our plans, our dispatches, before we even crossed the river." He told us how J. E. B. Stuart left the Confederate troops with no reconnoitering force. He saw the deaths of men he could name, heard the roar of the cannons in the quiet Pennsylvania hills. I saw his dead men littered across the field. I heard the crack of his rifles.

I wait for my father's card from Japan, his reaction to Hiroshima. He could send the picture postcard of the building they left as a memorial, but he won't. Maybe it will be a picture of the way Hiroshima looked sometime before August 6, 1945, or a card of the watch stopped at 8:16. My mother might send a picture of the shadows on the stones. When the bombs fell, the bodies of men and women who had been sitting on benches watching birds or the sunrise disintegrated from the heat of the blast, leaving only their shadows imprinted forever on the stone benches. For me, there is really only one picture of Hiroshima. In my father's magazines Hiroshima is the mushroom cloud billowing over the horizon.

I would like to get a picture of the Hiroshima maidens, the twelve or twenty women who were interviewed in a bombed-out hotel to see if they could be sent to New York for plastic surgery. I imagine them standing in line with their burned bodies, vying for a free trip to America where they could be reconstructed. I wonder what happened to the ones who were turned down. The Hiroshima maidens who came to New York lived in the homes of wealthy socialites while they waited for the bandages to be removed. When they returned to Japan they became models.

My father's card will be a picture of Hiroshima as it has been rebuilt. I will see new bars and hotels, modern office buildings. Pictures of progress and a denial that so much hatred can be loosed upon the world.

I wait and I imagine the postcard, but deep in my heart I hope he will not be able to write it. I hope he will not be able to put Hiroshima into words, place a foreign stamp on it, and stuff it into a Japanese mailbox. It is only a hope, my last hope for my father.

No Other Women

He is most often with me when I'm in bed with another man. In the last moments before sleep he strokes the long bones in my legs. We talk. Sometimes he tells me about an aviary he is designing or a book he is writing. We discuss politics, music, zoology. We agree what I am doing is nonsense.

In the past I had more control, but as I grow older he has come into his own. When I was a child he was malleable. He could be a cowboy, swirling a seagrass lariat over the necks of wild horses. Or a foreign dignitary wearing tailored clothes, gray pinstripe suits, soft lavender shirts. We flew open cockpit, carrying the mail to small midwestern wheat capitals. Slept on bright handmade quilts in the back of dingy Conestoga wagons. We ran guns for the Boers in 1899.

When I first imagined his life I wondered about his dog. An Afghan, long and beautiful, striding over a clover field, truly itself when running, looks vacant and pretentious at home. I was afraid he might like an Afghan; that disappointed me. A mottled dog is more his style, but not to his taste. He likes clean lines. At last we settled on a blue tick hound. Beautiful, useful, intelligent, patient. Last week he ran over it with the car.

As long as I can remember he has always been with me. When he bothers me I retaliate. Sometimes I go off with another man and break his heart. Often I kill myself in a car wreck or die of some incurable disease, pellagra, melancholia. Mostly I put him out of my mind.

I never used to bring him here but now I seem to have no choice. He dresses me, helps me style my hair in that fluffy way he thinks Salter liked so much. Makes me put on long skirts with a slit up the front exposing my calves and thighs when I sit on a bar stool. Other times he takes control of the car while we drive down the freeway to the grocery, the cleaners. He thinks blue jeans and unpainted eyes give me a casual appearance, as if I dropped in without plan. We come here, this bar I gave up visiting almost a year ago.

This is my lover's amusement, his revenge for the times I refused to take him along. Those times when I wouldn't think about him for days. Nothing escapes my lover; the smallest slights are repaid.

I don't see his car, my lover whispers.

He has other things to do, I reply.

Maybe he's home with the leper.

None of this was my idea; I wanted to go to town and buy some silver gourami for my freshwater tank. The evening was planned: a short trip to town for the fish I decided on last week. We could have picked up some Drambuie, built a fire against the chill of this mild summer rain, listened to Stravinsky, read. I should have known better; my lover has come to hate evenings like that. We either fight or, like this, end up looking for Salter. We've been here for the last three nights.

There's been a new bartender here for some time now. Kehoe was always very good about relaying messages. If he gave me my first drink on the house, I knew Kehoe and I would talk about sports, hockey was his favorite, and I would go home alone to listen to the laughter of my patient lover, his rebuke and scorn for this pitiful affair.

Kehoe tried to warn me: once the secrecy is gone you're headed for the end. They'll never leave their wives; it only means the fights begin. Kehoe was right. So was my lover.

Maggie and Louis sit in the back of the bar. They have met here for years. Salter and I used to play Scrabble with them on the small tables under the dim lights, listening to the quiet bar music and trying to think of words composed of the letters p, x, r, and u. Now I sit at the bar, do not look at Maggie and Louis. Sit with the other women, waiting.

This new bartender doesn't seem concerned. Perhaps there are no messages tonight. Maybe we were special to Kehoe. My lover used to tell me Kehoe was paid.

He'll come tonight, my lover whispers. I know he will. Tonight my lover drinks tequila. Competition puts him on edge.

There's a familiar tightness in my jawbones. Quietly drawing in the soft muscles of my stomach, arching my foot to tense my leg, I hear the triumphant laughter of my lover as Salter enters the bar. My lover drinks long from his endless empty glass while Salter comes slowly toward us.

"Nice to see you again." His soft voice, his hand on my shoulder.

He's waiting for someone else, my lover tells me.

"Expecting someone?" I ask.

"How about you?" Salter says with a smile.

That's no longer any of your business, Buddy, my lover tells him.

I smile. I want to be nice, to go over and talk to Maggie and Louis, have a game of Scrabble. I wonder if they still keep the board games under the bar.

Salter tells me he called a couple of weeks ago. He always tells me that now that we meet this way. I can hear my lover laugh; he gives a loud fart. He's been doing that lately. I seem to have no control over him anymore.

"How have you been?" I ask.

Salter was a mistake from the beginning. He looks nothing like the picture of my father taken in the fall of 1943 that my mother kept on her bureau all the years I was growing up. My mother said my father was killed in the war; my grandmother told me he ran away with a German woman just before I was born. In bars I talk to men who have daughters. I ask them how they treat their girls, what they want them to be when they grow up. A knowledgeable orphan has license.

Salter doesn't resemble my father, a man I have imagined based on an old photograph. Salter doesn't even have a daughter. We should never have started this; my lover is taking it much too seriously. Perhaps I should give my lover a hobby.

Ask Salter if she's dead yet, my lover whispers.

"How's your wife?" I say.

"About the same. The doctor gave her some new medication. It seems to be helping."

Tell him she is going to die anyway, my lover says. Tell him he is living with a corpse.

Salter asks if I've seen any new birds. He's a member of the National Audubon Society; we spent the weekends watching birds. Willets, ruddy turnstones, black-bellied plovers, oyster catchers. A new place every weekend. Evenings we sat in local mill bars listening to honky-tonk on the jukebox. Workingmen's bars like the ones Salter used to frequent as a young man growing up in Minnesota. Quiet nights in small motels, listening to the sounds of the surf, crickets, and night creatures warbling in the swamps. We planned to go out West, see ospreys and bald eagles. The biggest bird I ever saw was the American bittern.

I tell Salter I'm going down to the Gulf to collate a study for the Institute.

"Beautiful birds down there," he says. "Ibises, spoonbills. Look for the anhingas, snakebirds they're called. They swim practically submerged. Lower than grebes in the water."

Remind him of the chukars he promised to show you, Harlequin ducks. My lover can be a pain in the ass. Ospreys, he says.

"Really," I say. Only once in the past year have I gone bird watching. I saw nothing.

"Found a good Scrabble word," Salter says. "Zaxis. It's an axe with a three-dimensional coordinate system. Supposed to be rectangular."

Tell him you know his cock is getting hard, my lover says. Tell him you can feel the smooth skin on his butt.

"Twenty-one points," Salter says. "Not including double or triple squares."

"Maggie and Louis are here," I say.

Salter seems surprised, looks around from his bar stool to the tables hidden behind the piano and the jukebox. Maggie and Louis are gone. "I heard they were breaking up," he says.

Tell him you love to roll his balls between your fingers. Marbled eggs, sliding easily back and forth between your finger bones, around your palm.

"That was six, seven months ago," I remind him.

Salter stares at one of his own slightly mismatched eyes in the back bar mirror. I could never tell if he was almost wall-eyed or if one of his eyes was slightly crossed. His eyes cause him to tilt his head as if he has to look out of one or the other, never both at the same time.

Ask him why he threw you over for a corpse. Why he

chooses to spend his time with a dying woman. A woman who doesn't love him, can't take care of him. Has never been faithful.

Shut up! I tell my lover. I want to smash him, make him go away. Transform him into a cockroach and step on him, hear his brittle shell crack, the snap of his insect body beneath my leather sole.

"Did you get your promotion?" Salter asks.

"Yes," I respond. "Five months ago."

Ask him why he decided to *marry* the only white whore in eighty miles. Wanted to make a saloon girl, the whore with the heart of gold, go straight? A war profiteer into a housewife?

"Guess I forgot," Salter says. He waves to the bartender for more drinks.

"So how have you been?" Salter says after the drinks arrive.

"Fine."

Ask him why he supports a woman who buys fur coats she never wears. Why he pays her bills at I. Magnin's. Why he allowed her to bankrupt him five years ago buying stock in bogus radon mines in Montana.

Six, I tell my lover. You have forgotten a year has passed.

"Still live at the same place?" Salter asks.

"This is a pretty inane conversation, don't you think?"

"Can't we just be pleasant, have a nice discussion?"

"About the fact I haven't moved? Christ!" I want to be nice, take him to the Chinese place down the street, order wonton soup, talk about books, movies, my research project, his recent lawsuits. I used to love watching him in court.

You are obsessed with money, my lover says.

Go away, I tell him.

Face it, my lover says, his well-set grin flashing at me. You would hate a starving poet. The romance of living in a roach-infested garret, police locks anchored to the floorboards, would send you off to Bonwit's for forty-dollar peon shirts.

"Why can't we just be friendly toward one another?" Salter says, not looking at me. "Why all the nastiness every time we meet?"

Calmly I tell him I met a philatelist.

"Was he your father?"

"No. But he was interesting. Do you know the poor people of Kenya mail twopenny postcards with the same stamps that are auctioned in London for hundreds, thousands of pounds?"

Salter smiles. "You've been whoring around again."

"I think of it as sociology. Insurance people are the ones who bother me most." I tell him buying insurance is like placing your bets on the losing horse. If you get sick, your house burns down, someone steals your car, you're a winner. Otherwise you pay, month by month, in the hopes something will happen to you. Insurance people tell me this is an ignorant attitude in a civilized society.

"You've been whoring around again," Salter repeats.

"And what have you been doing? Masturbating?"

"Joyce needs me. She's having a rough time."

"That never used to bother you. You told me that in the beginning."

"Please be nice." His large gray eyes are looking at my face. I have never been able to see into men's eyes. The truth and honesty that supposedly lie there are obscured by the milky blue whites, flawed by the little red capillaries. I used to imagine the rods and cones were visible in the flecks of the irises, that I could see the mechanism that distinguishes light from dark. Beginning biology taught me rods and cones are microscopic.

My lover tells me Salter has another woman. More his

age, docile, yet charming and amusing. Qualities I have never been able to manage, he says.

Salter orders more drinks and a pack of Rolaids. Trying to be nice I ask Salter if his ulcer has been bothering him. He smiles, an attractive smile for a man who wears dentures. Normally when my lover and I search the bars I allow him a crooked smile or a broken tooth when we talk to men who wear dentures. It seems to give my lover character. But these days my lover has a mind of his own. Tonight he has adopted a boyish bucktoothed appearance. And a strawberry blonde mustache. Go away, I tell him. Let me be nice.

Salter is still looking at me. Perhaps I'm frowning, or yawning. I never seem to know what my face will do. It surprises me when I look in mirrors, seems to belong to someone else.

"Anything wrong?" Salter asks. "Can I help you?"

I refuse to tell him I miss his company on long afternoons, his talk, his friends. Maybe I will tell him about my lover. He might laugh. Salter has a lovely laugh.

My lover whispers in my ear, harsh, asthmatic. I smile; I have frightened him. It's been a long time since my lover was afraid. It's good for him.

Salter is still looking at my face. I feel my muscles moving minutely, the squint lines around my eyes, the pinched feeling near my nose. My face trying to be more beautiful in the bar lights.

Take him home, my lover says. Take him home! Lock him in the closet, the bathroom. I'll talk to him all day.

"I still have your Orvis bag," I say.

"Keep it. I've gotten another."

"Let's go to my house," I say. "I've got some ham I'll never finish. We'll have ham and Swiss on Jewish rye." He looks older somehow. A stranger's face I used to know so well.

Salter sighs. "Ham," he says. "Or a book you want to lend me. A record you want me to hear." Salter won't look at me. "You've got to give it up," he says at last.

My lover has a magic lantern show he runs at times like this. Sensual, lyrical music in the background. Soft lighting. Quiet scenes. Cooking and eating, reading in bed, driving long roads leading to isolated places, bird places. Small laughter, little touches. He swapped that for the leper, my lover says. He kisses her good-bye in the mornings, rubs her rotting bones to help her sleep at night. Some charming beautiful woman laughs in quiet motels with him. Makes plans. Harlequin ducks.

If I had changed, I start to tell my lover.

He cuts me off. Fool! He says. He wanted you in the beginning. It was different then. He would call. "Don't go to work today," he would say. "I can't wait to see you." Remember?

My lover is a poor mimic; Salter has a soft tenor. Besides, my lover says, I like you the way you are. Probably no one else does, but I do. Think about that. I never wanted you to frost your hair.

Salter orders one more drink, a bourbon and water for me. "I have to go," he says. His voice is very soft.

I smile at him, trying to be casual and easy. "It's rude to leave a lady sitting in a bar."

The bartender brings us the lone drink, sets it carefully on the white paper napkin in front of me. As he reaches for Salter's pile of bills and change, Salter signals for a drink for himself. He will have a drink with me. I know I have won.

There is no other woman, I tell my lover. He has only Joyce. My lover laughs and farts again. Methane gas, he says. Things that decompose, rot, die, give off gas. Methane gas.

Turning, Salter looks at a spot near the crown of my head. "You think all this important," he says, "but it's not."

•   •   •

"You mustn't think this wrong," Salter told me the last time he was at my house. We were standing by my tropical aquarium watching the delicate discus fish I breed move lazily, safely, through their artificial environment. In his hands he held the 200-mm telephoto lens I had just given him. A whim, a bribe. For photographing his birds, the shy egrets, black-crowned night herons that sneak away softly in the swamps.

"In the natural world," he said, "everything ends about like this." He told me about stress points in glass. Tapped a certain way, glass, rock, even people, he said, shatter. It seemed he did no more than touch the aquarium glass with the lens. And then he left through the front door, closing it quietly.

As the water gushed out of the twenty-gallon tank I picked up the telephoto lens, examined the prismatic cracks in the forged glass, watched the reflection of my face bounce back at me in cubistic angles. Later I vainly shuttled my dying discus into my holding tank, pots and pans in the kitchen. One male, a beautiful blue-green specimen with lovely yellow-orange borders, lived for two days.

"I should tell you a story," Salter says, "so you'll understand."

Make him read to you in bed, my lover urges. Pull the quilt up around your naked breasts, put your hand on his warm thigh. Leave on just the little light as you drink your Drambuie, smoke golden cigarettes in the near dark. Prove there is no other woman.

"One of my first battle assignments was taking the beach between Agana and Taumuming." Surprised, almost flattered,

I wonder why Salter wants to talk about the war. Another secret, the war.

It's a movie, my lover says. Just another old war story like the ones you've seen on TV all your life. A real American hero. Americans love World War II. Your father, my lover says, he was in the war.

Salter paints an exotic picture of tropical, humid Guam. Concrete Japanese pillboxes perched on the bluffs fifty feet above the beach. The boats were easy targets.

And John Wayne or William Holden was your captain, right? My lover lifts his lip in a sneer.

"It stalled," Salter says. Salter tells me about the men on board his landing craft hit with pieces of shrapnel, deadly little splinters of the boat cutting through an arm, an eye.

My lover laughs. Now he's going to tell you he saw God.

"A dead hit," Salter says. He wants me to know about shock waves in the water. How the landing craft disintegrated, disappeared. Transformed into fire, flying metal birds that shot away out of sight.

"I made it to the beach, no farther."

That's what you get for being a halfwit, Buddy. While your guts roasted on the sand, I had a paid vacation in Zurich.

Moving slowly on his bar stool, Salter faces me, his mismatched eyes not looking at my face. Perhaps he is still seeing the beach at Guam, or maybe he is staring at my lover. I'm afraid to look. Salter talks about the stinking scattered debris on the beach. Soldiers and coconut shells split open. Watching gecko lizards with translucent suction pads on the ends of their toes as they crawled over dead soldiers. He says he hoped he would be killed by the Japanese, rather than eaten alive by the geckos and scaly iguanas. He watched their sharp teeth with needlelike points slicing through the scrotum of the body lying next to him.

Now tell us all about how you wanted to have children. That's why you married the whore, the leper. Right, Buddy? First white woman you saw, married her drunk on the spot, hoping she would pop you a brat. Prove you are not a lizard. My lover laughs drunkenly, swaying on his bar stool.

"Women and children are innocent and ignorant," Salter says. "They never go to war."

We finish our drinks in silence and again Salter signals for just one more, a bourbon and water for me. "I have to go," he says. He rests his hand briefly on my shoulder as he stands to leave.

My lover laughs. I bet the new one is a blonde, has long frosted blonde hair.

I would like to fight with Salter, cause a scene. Watching his back, the narrow hips in his tailored suit, I want to stop him before he reaches the door. Talk to him, pull his hair.

My lover winks and gives me a generous smile. In the days of liberation, he says, we ought to have a program for all male heroes. "King for a Day." You know the type.

A man and a woman are at a table near the door. I forget the man's name. Salter puts a hand on his shoulder; the man turns his head up. They smile, shake hands. I want to pull Salter's hair, bloody his nose. Salter stands, talking to that man, his back toward me.

The guy'll be a janitor for twenty-three years in the Empire State Building. He's got a junkie son, a daughter with cystic fibrosis. My lover laughs at his own fantasy.

The man and the woman, Salter, they all laugh. I will keep my glass in my fist, turn him around with the palm of my hand. Pulling my arm back, I will hit him with all my strength, the glass in my fist for power. He will wander his fancy law courts with a swollen nose and blue-black eyes, faded greens and yellows on his face while the bruises heal.

My lover crosses his eyes and weaves around the barroom floor, his legs locked together at the knees, hands and arms splayed out from his body. He begins to drool.

Waving at them, Salter starts again toward the door. A Kabuki dancer with long red lines scratched down his face, the Japanese symbol for tears.

He's black, our hero is, and his wife's last baby was white. Now he's got wax lung from polishing the fifteenth floor too long.

My lover laughs and returns to his bar stool. And based on the applause meter, he says, Monty Hall is going to award him an Esther Williams swimming pool he can install on the rooftop of his tenement.

My lover laughs and winks again. He has always had a nice laugh.

Salter is gone. In the silence of the bar music I listen for the slam of a car door, the whine of the engine.

I have no choice. I would rather do this outside, maybe in the country. A bright dawn with sparkling lawns, the firing squad at attention. Polished brass buttons on serious blue uniforms with gray stripes running down the outside leg of the trousers. But there is no time. There is no firing squad.

I believe a double on the rocks will help. Wild Turkey, I down it almost neat. Before my head starts to spin I focus all my attention on my lover. I look over his American movie star features, the easy smile from central casting. Listen to his laugh, very melodious now. Look deeply into his vacant eyes; there is no sign of terror or fear. I have never known how much he knows about me, my thoughts, my mind. A stranger's face I used to know so well.

Your father, he says, he could win a swimming pool.

•   •   •

My lover takes a long drink from his glass. While his eyes are averted I begin. Concentrating, I slowly melt him back into what he actually is, the thin air I breathe. In the aquavideo of this dark bar I unmold his animated synthesized form. He loses his glass as his fingers begin to stretch, drip away from his hands. His arms, legs, oozing away from him slowly. Only his eyes seem to hold. Viscous, like pouring tar or warm honey, his shoulders, his mouth sag away from the sparkling green eyes. He is composed of new colors, colors I see only in my sleep. He tries to compose himself, reconstruct himself. But the melting bones in his hands and arms merely tear away, drip into an opaque puddle on the floor.

His eyes are last, staring at me. They seem to be laughing, dancing slowly down through the air like racing raindrops on a window pane.

I see his life. I forgive his lies. My father was not a pimp for the Mafia, a mercenary, an embezzler. When I was a child this lover read me stories in the dark as I tried to fall asleep. Drew pictures on the steamy mirror in the bathroom. Invented puzzles, games. Manufactured futures and dreams. Helped me run away from home and told me where to go so I would be found when my mother was no longer angry, merely thankful I was safe. With the high school boys in the backseat of parked cars he helped me unhook my bra, assured me it was all right to take off my pants. Guided our hands as the boys entered me.

He held my stomach and head when I was sick, put his arms around me when I cried. My perfect lover, stroking me gently, ploughing me unmercifully. He put babies in my belly and made them disappear. He selected the men in the bars.

And we talked. On buses, in bed, all the quiet places. We saw American Indians before the missionaries, the death of Anne Boleyn. Lenin kissed my hand.

I order another shot of Wild Turkey. Somewhere in the back of the bar I hear him singing *Blue Suede Shoes* in imitation of Elvis Presley. Tomorrow we must pick up the silver gourami. I wonder if I would look younger with frosted hair.

Miss Buick of 1942

Albums

She still feels the long chiffon gown, the silk lining next to her skin, damp with the moisture of excitement. Rhinestones glitter on spaghetti straps, small bats of light in the corners of her eyes. Her shoulders are bare but powdered. Her memory is a dream of herself, colored photographs that linger in her mind. Memories of scents, textures to touch in her thoughts, posed like the 8 x 10 glossy photographs she keeps in the three leather albums.

She sees herself standing in the spotlights beneath the banners of the Buick Motor Company marquee. In her arms are the roses and from her hand dangle the silver keys to the burgundy red 1942 Buick that will take her across the country for a year. She will travel to places she has never seen, Oregon, Oklahoma, a smile on her lips and the blood red Buick around her, her name in gold along its sides. She holds the roses, curling the corners of her eyes to pierce the spotlights, trying to see her aunt and uncle somewhere in the hall, clapping, smiling. It will be different for her now after this August night in 1941. They told her she must learn to drive.

Miss Buick wears her tiara, reclining in a two-piece white bathing suit on the hood of the burgundy Buick as it bakes on a gray sandy beach. The tiara glitters in the noonday sun and in this photo her blonde hair is crowned with reflected white stars. There is a photo for each state in the first leather album, forty-eight pictures of herself and the car. New Mexico, in a yellow halter top and navy blue shorts she straddles the thick neck of a Brahma bull, a cowboy's hat upon her head, her back braced against the hump. The points of the boned horns reach to the edge of the camera's frame and the hollow eyes of the bull are as red as the Buick in the background.

Driving at 35 mph to save gas for the war, her aunt and uncle taking turns behind the wheel, Miss Buick dreamed of Gloria, her sister. It was Gloria who should have worn the tiara, Gloria who was groomed for this life. Gloria the singer, the actress, the model. Gloria who was going to be a star. Gloria was pouring a shot of Puerto Rican rum into paper cup Cokes as her boyfriend drove the 1938 Packard into the front of a fully loaded coal truck rounding a blind bend in Pennsylvania. They were on their way to New York to sing show tunes to men going overseas. Miss Buick has not learned to drive. Her aunt and her uncle appear in only one shot, standing in the snow outside the munitions factory in Vermont, looking off somewhere outside the frame. Miss Buick remembers how the cold burned the inside of her nose as she stood beside the big red car, the smell of cordite and wire in the air.

In the picture of Washington the Straits of Juan de Fuca glisten behind the Buick. Vancouver Island is in the background. Miss Buick likes that one particularly. She wears a WAC's uniform, her hand drawn up in salute, a glimpse of another country over her shoulder. For the Virginia picture Miss Buick reclines on the hood of the Buick as a hoist raises the car to the deck of a battleship docked in the quay of Newport News. Beneath this picture is a speech written for her, her signature large across the bottom in a clear neat hand.

In the spotlight again Miss Buick is caught at the moment she lifts the sparkling tiara from her own blonde head, begins to pass it to a coiffed brunette who is even now crying, waiting and crying for the tiara to be placed upon her curls. In her hand, the coiffed brunette dangles the silver keys to the brand new emerald green 1943 Buick, barely visible behind the two women, dwarfed by the wing of an airplane.

The second album contains amateur snapshots of someone she no longer knows. A young woman stands in the orange groves outside Tallahassee, her aunt and uncle flanking her sides. Their arms are loaded with fat oranges, they laugh into the lens. A Boston bull terrier, black and white with a full square jaw and slightly bowed legs, stares into the camera out of small eyes set far back to the sides of its head. There are feet and legs in this picture, in the center a pair of bright red shoes on long narrow feet too large to be fashionable. Page after page in this album displays snapshots of couples, each couple not quite the same. A tall blonde woman in a green cloche hat stands next to an Army general, his arm draped over her shoulder. She dances with an Air Force lieutenant, the bill of his hat shadowing his face. Standing beside a naval officer in dress blues, she wears a flounced skirt of many layers, ruffles lying above her breasts. The last picture is a shot of her profile, the blonde hair almost gone brown, a yellow canary with wings aflutter balances on the edge of her finger.

The third album is marked, dates on every picture. June 2, 1945, she stands in a long white lace dress, the veil, a bouquet of lilies of the valley and white tea roses. Beside her in a dark tuxedo with a cummerbund of his family's ancestral tartan plaid, stands the electrical engineer, an electrical architect who can design the lighting systems for streets and office buildings, arrange the energy flow in dams and ships at sea. In black ink under this photo are penned the words: *bright future*.

April 12, 1950, she stands in front of a new brick home, neighboring houses set equally back from the street are barely visible at the edge of the frame. On either side of the concrete walk stand two sapling maples, five feet tall. In the front of the round arched door she holds a bundle of baby blankets in her arms, her legs strong and smooth beneath the new linen skirt. She feels the coolness of the nylons on her legs, cannot remember what happened to that beige skirt.

Linda

Miss Buick gave Linda her fox-headed stole, glass beads for the eyes, the mouths clamped to the tails of the next one on the line. Linda learned to count. There were seven little foxes on the stole, their tiny feet hanging free from the body of fur. Linda slept with the foxes, cuddling her baby's face next to the hard glass eyes, the tiny ivory teeth. Linda said she was Gloria Swansdown, Beronica Lake, a mysterious woman named Miff Smiff. She said she lived in a California castle and all her furs were real. Minks curled around her neck and ate out of her hand, their tails brushing the lobes of her ears.

The engineer bought a Philco television, giant black-green screen, big brass knobs. On Saturday nights they picnicked, ate hot dogs, soft white buns, canned baked beans, seated on the living room floor in front of the Philco. The Lone Ranger, Hopalong Cassidy, the Cisco Kid. Linda counted eleven dead men and was pleased to remember the number. Eleven, the only truly original number in her collection. She went to bed before Groucho Marx but crept back downstairs and peeked through the bannisters, giving herself away when she squealed at the duck dropping into the screen at the sound of a loud brassy horn.

All the pictures of Linda belong in the third leather album each dated in a clear neat hand. May 14, 1952, Miss Buick is in pedal pushers kneeling in wild flowers growing in sunlight. She holds a bouquet out to her daughter. Wild daisies, asters, a few blue pansies. Linda's knees are caked with mud, her little hands reaching out for the flowers. August 23, 1955, Miss Buick wears a one-piece bathing suit with plastic bones under the cups and holds Linda by the hand as they stand ankle deep in the surf. The Steel Pier is in the background. December 25, 1959, Miss Buick and Linda sit in front of the tree, glitter of tinsel and Christmas balls against the dark green needles. Artificial lighting for indoor photos creates halos above their hair.

Pictures We Do Not See

Miss Buick sat in the front seat of the Oldsmobile, clenching and unclenching her long, ringed fingers, trying to restore circulation to them. Linda sat beside her reading a Donald Duck comic book, on her lap a stack of others, Mickey Mouse, Popeye, Goofy, and Pluto. At the bottom of the pile was the thick twenty-five-cent Gene Autry special, a present from the engineer she was saving for last. Each year they traveled in the Oldsmobile to a vacation spot, sometimes the seashore, sometimes the mountains. Always somewhere away from home. The engineer talked of driving to California and Miss Buick remembered all the roads, changed somehow in the last few years, but knew them nevertheless. She knew Richmond, Virginia, was directly east of Kansas City, Missouri, that the quickest way to Chicago was through Toledo, Ohio.

Clenching and unclenching her hands, she watched the knuckles whiten with pressure. Inside her left ear she listened to a moth and a high-pitched whistle, the moth fluttering and beating against her eardrum, the whistle playing like a tune.

They drove a mountain road, 50 mph, beige sandstone cliffs to the left, green maples and beeches trailing away from the road cut, sloping down the talus toward a rocky stream. Miss Buick watched the black asphalt patches disappear beneath the wheels of the car, saw small animals and children scuttle toward the road, to be trapped and flattened by the tires. Women and old men dart out onto the pavement, the car floats over the retaining wall, drifts noiselessly through space to land upside down in the rocky black stream, to burst into flame.

The ringing grew louder, the moth beating more breathlessly inside her ear. Her lower arms prickled with pins and needles of numbness. Rounding a curve, Miss Buick snatched at the hem of her daughter's dress, flipped the skirt up over Linda's eyes, held it tightly around the crown of the little girl's head. The comic books bunched in the child's lap; the rough paper tickled her face. With her eyes squeezed shut against the impending crash, Miss Buick held her daughter for a moment more, released her slowly with a sigh.

"Why, Mommy?"

"I didn't want you to see."

"See what?"

"Gloria died rounding a curve."

The engineer said: "Oh for Christ's sake."

Linda loved birds. Together she and Miss Buick bought a cedar birdhouse and matching feeder, five pounds of wild birdseed and a full color guide to birds of North America. They hung the birdhouse and feeder in a maple just outside the kitchen window. The maple stood twelve feet tall; in the summer it cast an almost full circle of shade. They made a special trip to the stationery store to buy a bound book with blank pages. Linda drew a picture of each bird on the separate white sheets. Starlings, bluejays, house sparrow, red-breasted nuthatch, catbird, brown thrasher, tufted titmouse, evening grosbeak. There were plenty of pages left in the book for the birds that had not yet arrived. They raced to see who could record the most sightings; they were almost even on the cardinal page. Linda had forty-seven sightings, Miss Buick forty-two. A pair of eastern bluebirds nest in the cedar house for three years. Their cat, Toll House Cookie, ate the female that third spring.

Home Snapshots

Miss Buick discovered the beauties of old brick. In women's magazines she saw page after page of full color photographs showing sunny rooms with sturdy furniture under patterned slipcovers, walls of old brick, railroad tie beams spaced evenly across ceilings. The three of them made a fifty-mile trip in the Oldsmobile to the site of an abandoned mill soon to be torn down. The brick was expensive; the engineer said they could afford only part of a wall. The contractor owned a '42 Buick for almost six years. Best car he ever owned and he always bought Buicks. A Buick customer for thirty-five years. For an extra $20 he had his son split the bricks with a special saw that was rarely used. Not much call for half a brick, he said.

The electrical engineer took pictures with the new Polaroid Land camera they gave him for Christmas. Miss Buick and Linda stand in the kitchen before the white porcelain stove and refrigerator, the bare blank wall behind them. The top of Linda's head is even with her mother's shoulder. They disconnected the gas pipe, moved the refrigerator away from the wall, a blank plaster wall with small grains of sand swirled into circular designs. There was a dark line that followed the contoured shadows where the stove and refrigerator stood.

They worked after school. Each evening the electrical engineer took another Polaroid snapshot. Miss Buick and Linda, in old aprons and slacks, mixing up mortar for the wall. Miss Buick and Linda, half a brick and trowels in their hands, the wall almost to their waists. Linda on a ladder placing a premortared brick neatly along a line close to the ceiling, Miss Buick holds the ladder and looks up at her.

There are nine pictures. Each evening after the picture was taken the three of them ate at Howard Johnson's. Miss Buick had roast turkey, bread stuffing, thin whipped potatoes nine nights in a row. She said she could never eat enough roast turkey.

There is a final picture of Miss Buick and Linda. Miss Buick is dressed in a blue wool suit with a boxlike jacket. Linda smiles at her side in a green plaid skirt and a yellow sweater. She is wearing her first pair of nylons and heels. The wall is finished, the stove and refrigerator are back in place, gleaming white against the brick wall that looks black in the poor lighting.

Education

Seated behind the wheel of the new 1962 Oldsmobile Miss Buick turned the key in the ignition. While the big car idled she stared at the dash, not looking at the electrical engineer who nodded and smiled beside her as he explained each gear again. She could not hear him, a moth beating in her ear. He demonstrated again with his feet dancing above the floorboards what the steps would be to use the clutch and the brake. He reached over and pushed the gear shift along the column, explaining each gear and what it did. Sitting in the Oldsmobile in the driveway by the side of the house, Miss Buick looked back over her shoulder to the road sloping away.

She let out the clutch with her left foot, pushed hard on the brake with her right. The Oldsmobile stalled and the engineer said: Let's try it again. He moved his feet above the floorboards once more, lit another Camel and blew the first cloud of smoke at Miss Buick, talked of timing and why she should learn. She turned the key in the ignition, pumped the gas with her foot. The engine raced, the engineer said: Not like that. She pushed at the clutch with her left foot, felt the car drift down the driveway toward the street. Her right foot found the brake, jerked the Oldsmobile to a stop.

Miss Buick's knuckles were white, the bands of her rings biting into her fingers, her palms, as her hands clutched at the wheel. Let's try it again, the engineer said, and he pulled on his Camel in short bursts. Inside her left ear the moth beat a tattoo, a high, whistling sound near her brain. She turned the ignition key and felt the car drifting again, drifting back toward the street. She shifted to reverse, stepped hard on the brake. The Oldsmobile stalled in the driveway.

They had drifted almost to the curb for the second time that morning. The engineer said: Let's try forward. Go back up the drive and we'll do it again. Miss Buick's shoulders were damp against the vinyl seat; there was a cramp in her left leg below the knee.

The engineer moved the gear shift to the forward position. Miss Buick turned the key in the ignition, her left foot standing down upon the clutch. The Oldsmobile drifted back toward the road. Miss Buick pushed hard on the gas, remembered to lift her foot from the clutch. The Oldsmobile raced up the drive and Miss Buick screamed. The engineer reached for the wheel, the brake. The right headlight and fender caught the side of the garage, splintering wood against blue metal and shiny chrome. The Oldsmobile stopped, stalled, as the engineer pushed the gear shift into neutral.

The engineer switched off the ignition and told Miss Buick to get out of the car. His door smashed shut, the engineer crawled across the seat, got out of the Oldsmobile on the driver's side.

"It's only a month old," the engineer said. Miss Buick was crying.

"I don't want to drive it," she said.

"You don't have to wreck it if you don't want to drive it. This will send our insurance up."

"We could have gone somewhere flat."

"You didn't have to wreck it."

"This was your idea."

"Can't you do anything right by yourself?"

From the window of her room Linda saw her mother crying, her father walking away. It was always like this, for no reason.

Under the eaves in the attic Linda found Miss Buick's birds. Pigeons and sparrows and swallows. In corners and under the vents Linda discovered the holes cut out of the insulation, the boards pried apart with the claws of a hammer. In secret Linda watched as Miss Buick saved breadcrumbs and nuts, dug worms out of their garden. Linda stood in the attic and waited for the birds to parade around her feet, bobbing their heads up and down. Some fluttered in the air around her head, but she never brought food like her mother. In the night she believed she could hear them walking overhead, their tiny nails tapping on the ceiling.

Seated on the couch in the middle of the afternoon Linda found Miss Buick crying. She heard boots in the attic and waited for the men to come down. They wore masks on their faces and carried sacks in their arms as they walked to their truck in the driveway. With the sounds of Miss Buick's sobs in her ears Linda mounted the stairs to the attic. Fresh mortar filled the holes, pink plugs stopped up the insulation. In the far corner she found one bird, a sparrow on its back, wings spread. The tiny beak was open and Linda saw its tongue.

In the evening the engineer came home from his job. "It's done," he said. "There'll be no more of it."

The House

There was mail every day, for Linda, her folders. Sometimes she would sit with her coffee upon the front step and wait for the mailman, a dollar she had taken from Miss Buick hidden in her pocket to give to the mailman for stamps. Stamps for letters to travel agencies, for more posters and folders, brochures and maps. Venezuela, Cairo, the bell tower at Notre Dame. Pictures of Mount Fuji and city maps of Sidney. Folders in Turkish with English translations that tell of the wonders of Istanbul.

From ten to eleven she sat in her room. With sharp nail scissors and thin clear tape she cut out the pictures of men round the world. She followed the lines of their jaws, the waves of their hair. The ones that were barefoot she cut off their toes. If they held hands with a woman she cut off their arms. She disliked posters printed on both sides. The pictures overlapped, a man on the front with tennis shorts, a man on the back in a dinner jacket. She could never decide; she threw them both away.

With the folders cut and the scraps folded neatly in strips Linda taped the men to her wall. She arranged them as a map of the world, Orientals to the left, Nordics to the right. The Latins and Africans taped down by the floor, the Americans right in the middle. There were spots in the map, places she could not fill. She had no Eskimos to be taped near the ceiling. There was no one to tape in Atlantis. Russians were a problem, no one traveled the Steppes. Each day she replaced the thin Indian bedspread that covered her wall, covered her map of the world.

In the afternoons they cleaned. Mondays the living room, Tuesdays the kitchen, Wednesdays the bathroom, Thursdays the bedroom where Miss Buick and the engineer slept. On Fridays they cleaned Linda's room. She lifted the madras bedspread to show her mother her wall. They admired the new ones, wondered where to get folders for Tierra del Fuego, how a picture of Lapland would fit. Linda said she would need a new wall soon.

Just before dinner they worked in the garden. Tomatoes and corn, cauliflower and beans, radishes, onions and peas. Miss Buick believed in being prepared. They canned fruits and vegetables in season. In the evenings the engineer admired their food. He wanted to know if they were happy.

The Detective

In a glassine case in the detective's wallet were the last two pictures of Linda. They were pulled from a file marked *Runaways, Missing Persons*. The first picture is of Linda at her high school graduation. She stands in a long black gown, a golden tassel flipped over one eye. Behind her is the high school, other black figures in robes. Under the picture someone has printed the words: *Graduation, June 5, 1967*. The printing is small and neat. There is another picture of Linda with the same hairdo and smile surrounded by new red luggage. She is wearing a straight skirt and matching sweater; her feet are clad in simple black pumps. She is leaving to go off to college.

The electrical engineer gave these pictures to the police. Fuzzy images of Linda, her smile, copied out line by line on police telexes in seventeen states when Linda failed to come home for Christmas, December 1968. Two pictures and the letter she sent in her absence, the letter said only: *There are things I must do for myself.*

It was snowing, the temperature in the mid-teens, when Miss Buick and the engineer received the Polaroids. The first one was a crowd shot, young people gathered around a banner that read STOP THE WAR. START THE REVOLUTION. Miss Buick had never seen these people before, long-haired boys, girls in tight blue jeans. The second picture was of three people, handcuffed, marching into a building. Two boys and a girl in a long red dress. Their heads are down, a police nightstick waves in the air above them. Miss Buick stared at the nightstick and thought of birds without wings. In the third picture a girl stands barefoot in the snow of a big city park, a monument rising behind her. She is dressed in a long red robe, her hair is cropped short, golden loops hang from her ears. In her hand is a piece of fruit, an avocado or pear. The girl neither laughs nor smiles. She looks directly into the camera, no expression upon her face. Underneath this snapshot are typed the words: *February 17, 1969. New York City.*

The Road

In a cardboard box next to an old china doll lie photographs of Miss Buick's childhood. There is a posed family portrait of a mother and father holding two infant daughters. Somewhere in this stack is a hand-colored photo of Gloria dressed in a sailor's suit, the only picture that is not of a couple or group. Miss Buick as a child is never alone. She sits on a swing tied to a weeping willow, her aunt standing behind with hands on the swing chains ready to push. Miss Buick sits on the lap of her father, his head somewhere outside the frame, a brown baby rabbit held tight in her hands as it waits for the eyedropper of milk. A group of children play house, Gloria dressed as the bride in a floppy white hat and long dress with the waist just touching her hips. Miss Buick is dressed as the baby.

On top of the box and the old china doll Miss Buick places her three leather albums, the trophy, and the sparkling tiara. She packs these things in a new red satchel, hefts the weight of it with her left hand. It is Monday and Miss Buick should dust end tables, sweep under chairs. In the garden she must thin the peas, weed the beans, prune sucker shoots off the tomatoes. It is warm as Miss Buick walks the road away from her house, shifting her red satchel from shoulder to shoulder. A boy on a motorcycle whistles; his hair is as long as Linda's and blows away from his face as he rides.

The trucks look like ships, sampans she saw once in a movie, moored to the shiny gas pumps floating in the black asphalt of the truck stop parking lot. Miss Buick feels the heat of the pavement through the soles of her shoes, the warmth of the sun on her naked legs under the white cotton skirt. On tiptoes, she can not see into the cabs, only radios and visors stretching across the truck's ceiling. She has heard men can live in these trucks, little beds in the back, dangerously close to the fuel tanks. Pacing off the front of the truck, three strides, Miss Buick decides truckers must sleep in a ball, their legs curled up to their chests as they rest.

Inside, women pour coffee, truckers eat pie. Two soldiers sit at a booth by the door, a map spread open before them and duffle bags lying at their feet. There is music on the jukebox, the kind Linda always liked. A woman's voice sings over the clatter of dishes. The menu describes Four Wheelers, Trucker's Special, the Big Ten Four. Miss Buick handles a cream pitcher shaped like a cow and stares at the full color poster of Miss Snap-On Tools of 1971, dressed in a pale yellow bikini encircled by a star of bright metal wrenches. Miss Buick decides the young woman's teeth are capped, the smile a little crooked like Gloria's.

Miss Buick pours cream from the cow's mouth into her white steaming mug and she waits, not quite sure what to do. A man sits down beside her and Miss Buick wonders if he is a trucker, stares at him out of the corner of her eye. He looks more like a cowboy than a trucker to her, high-heeled boots with pointed toes, blue denim jeans, and a bright red flannel shirt. His hair is cropped short, unlike most of the boys she sees these days, boys thin and pale with long silky hair. The type of boys Gloria always liked. In New Mexico Miss Buick met cowboys who dressed like this man and remembered cowboys drove trucks. One of them asked her if Buick made pickups and they laughed, the sound of their voices still in her ears.

"You live around here?" the trucker asks.

Miss Buick smiles the trained grin, pleased with his question but more pleased with the answer she can give. "I did," she says and pats the red satchel at her feet. "But now I am traveling. I know all the roads. I've been all over the country."

"Me too," the trucker says. "I haul crude oil from Illinois."

Packed in her red satchel Miss Buick has the Illinois picture in the first leather album. She stands in a red dress and white pumps beside the '42 Buick. Above her is a banner that reads SUPPORT OUR BOYS ABROAD. BUY AMERICAN. *Buy Buick*. The low hills of Illinois roll back from the car, in the distance is a white farmhouse.

"I'm going to get a truck," Miss Buick says. "With a truck I can find my daughter."

"What kind of rig?"

"What kind are there?"

"Mack. Roadway. Peterbilt. I got a GMC myself."

Miss Buick smiles. "Peter Built? How nice."

"Just a truck, lady. Been in business longer than me. What's a truck got to do with your daughter?"

"She left to do things for herself. And I know there are things I should do. I'm going to learn to drive a truck. To move things up to Alaska. We've never been to Alaska."

"Good money in Alaska," the trucker says. "But you don't need a truck to get there."

"No cars," Miss Buick says. "A new car each year just looks good in the driveway. I want to do something useful." In a truck, driving a truck, Miss Buick could haul vegetables from their garden. They could sing show tunes as they drive into another country.

"My wife's a nurse," the trucker says. "That's useful. Good money too."

"My daughter wouldn't be a nurse. She's moving, doing things. In a truck I could find her. We could go to Alaska. She's never been to Alaska." Miss Buick and Linda could live in a truck, sleep curled up in balls, their legs tucked to their breasts, driving the Canadian road to Alaska like birds heading north for the summer.

"Your husband think this is a good idea?"

"He can light ships at sea, turn water into electrical power. This is just for Linda and me. In Alaska birds change color with the seasons."

"Alaska's no place for women alone. I wouldn't let my wife go up there."

"I have all we need." Miss Buick pats the satchel at her feet. "Linda should have this. She left before I could tell her."

"No place for a woman," the trucker says again. "But there's plenty of work, I know that."

"That's just what we need," says Miss Buick. "That and a truck we can live in."

"You should have a nice house, not a greasy old truck."
He laughs at Miss Buick's idea.

"It's work that we need, not houses. In a truck we could
drive to Alaska."

Rising, the trucker pays for his meal and returns to his rig
in the lot. Miss Buick continues to sit at the counter and sip
coffee, pleased with the notion she can sit there all day, a full
cup of coffee before her. She thinks of Alaska and living in a
truck, watching birds migrate along the western flyway.

In her house down the road Miss Buick has left one picture, a photograph taken in her childhood. She sits in a white
pony cart, a parasol shading her face. A red-liveried Negro
drives the horse along the lane, seagulls wheel in the air above
them. In a small neat hand she has penned: *There are things I
must do for myself.*

Perhaps the childhood was happy.

Perhaps only the child was sad.

The Crane Wife

_____

As the winter dragged on Nadia began to understand why happily married women take lovers they don't really care about. Since New Year's Day she and her husband Ted had spent only four days together, and Nadia found herself thinking of him as if he belonged to another woman. Perhaps Ted really married his career, in love with the chaotic politics of Central America and the fast, dangerous music afloat in the humid air. Ted would be gone at least another three weeks, and Nadia was tempted to hop the first plane to Peking, Warsaw, Istanbul. Any place where she didn't speak the language.

Today was the worst blizzard yet, the Arctic itself cutting across all of New England. Nadia curled in the bed with Cody, their tortoiseshell cat, noticing ice on the inside of the bedroom window and worried about a bubbling cough coming up from the furnace.

In her old chenille robe and slippers she looked out front for the paper and watched the thick veil of falling snow, wondering how icy the roads would be. There was no paper, or at least she couldn't find it, and if she didn't shovel the walk there would be no mail. The plows had been through and piled the gritty stuff up over the curb and onto the sidewalk, chunks of dirty ice lying about like broken glass. She thought of Ted under a hot tropical sun, the winged pattern of sweat staining the back of his khaki shirt, his curly hair dripping dark ringlets.

She fixed coffee and headed for her small office, a converted bedroom at the back of the house, and the computer for her word-processing business. The room looked out over the patio and yard. At first she didn't register what she saw. She thought it was some aberration caused by the flat light of the storm. But it drew her to the window, and as she peered out it moved its head and blinked a golden eye at her.

It stood in the lee of the house sheltered from the wind. It seemed calm and curious at the same time, moving its head from side to side to look through the window. The bird was immense, standing eye level with her. Its long black neck undulated in a graceful S curve down to the white body. The top of its head was a bright red cap, the only spot of color on the black and white bird. It paced back and forth on its thin gray legs and Nadia could see its tracks, troughs really, all across her patio, rapidly filling with snow. Suddenly it tapped its long, rapierlike bill against the glass, and she jumped, amazed and surprised by the noise.

A huge bird. She'd watched hawks soaring on thermals, flushed grouse while walking through the woods. This black-and-white bird with the odd red cap set like a yarmulke on the top of its head stepped around the patio on its stilt legs. Its shape reminded her of a gigantic egret, oversized like a cartoon. It continued peering at her through the glass, cocking its head from side to side as if one eye or the other would translate what it saw into some bird knowledge or reaction.

It moved back a few paces on the porch and suddenly spread its immense wings, black-tipped, and held them out as if to embrace the air. It bobbed and bowed its head a few times, and if it had been a person Nadia felt this would have been a greeting. It refolded its wings, then spread them again, repeating the bobbing and bowing. It did not fly away, but strutted up and down the patio opening and closing its wings. The great wing span made it look like an angel perched on swizzle sticks, feathered wings dipped in ink.

Drawing her robe close around her throat Nadia went to the back door and opened it slowly. She wasn't sure exactly what she intended to do. The sight of the bird strutting across her patio was comical, yet part of her wanted to see those long wings take flight and soar over the rooftops and treeline. She wished this were a trained bird and would fly over the snowy yard and come back to her like a remote-controlled model plane.

Her feet, covered only with her furry bedroom slippers, went instantly numb as she stepped out onto the patio. The bird opened its wings again, then fanned them forward, their tips nearly touching. Throwing them back, like stretching after a good sleep, it bared its chest to her, showing off its pure white breast. It arched its long neck and opened its beak and emitted a cry. "Crew-whip!"

"Hello," Nadia said, then laughed at herself. Talking to an ostrich, or whatever this bird was. She knew it wasn't an ostrich, or any common bird. She'd seen great blue herons fishing in streams. Perhaps this was a great black-and-white heron, although she wasn't sure there was such a bird. The great blue heron had been big-bird-size, but this monster towered over any bird she'd ever seen, with the exception of ostriches in zoos. She wondered if it could fly, why it hadn't flown away when she opened the back door.

The phone rang. The bird seemed to hear it too, and folded its wings and craned its neck in the direction of the house. "Whip."

"The phone," Nadia said, talking to this bird the way she talked to Cody, the cat. Moving slowly so as not to frighten it she backed off the patio and into the kitchen, leaving the door open to the cold and snow blowing in so she could keep an eye on the bird. She didn't want to miss seeing it fly away.

The phone sounded its fourth ring as Nadia answered. "Hello," she whispered, so as not to startle the bird, which now moved toward the open door, following her.

"Speak up. I never get a good connection down here."

"Ted." His voice was quite loud in her ear. The big black-and-white bird stood framed by the kitchen doorway.

"How are you? I miss you."

"Where are you now?" The bird kept its bright eye on her, swiveling its head from side to side, its neck stretched out as it peered into the house. The wind lifted and ruffled the long black feathers of its tail.

"I'm in St. Lucia, some island in the West Indies off the coast of Venezuela. I'm afraid I've got some bad news. Everything's stalled down here. I'm going to knock out a quick piece on coffee growers and then go back and see if anything's changed. This story just might take longer than I thought."

"It's awfully cold here," Nadia said. "I haven't turned the radio on but I bet we're having a snow emergency. The paperboy didn't deliver the paper this morning." Had he ever had an assignment that didn't take longer than he thought it would? She'd married the telephone and the mailbox, not Ted.

The big black-and-white bird took a step into the kitchen.

"Are you all right? Car work OK?"

She could tell him about the bird. "Yeah, I'm fine. But with this storm I don't think I'll use the car. I've finished Federman's bibliography, all 842 entries, but I've still got lots of work." She kept her eye on the white bird, whooping crane, she guessed, and then wondered if whooping cranes were extinct. She'd never seen one in New England before.

"There's more to do on the Nicaragua piece but I'm

burnt," Ted said. "This little coffee junket will give me a break before I have to tie it all off."

"That'll be nice." Her eyes locked with those of the white bird, drawing it across her kitchen. Its nails ticked against the wooden floor.

"I'll call you when I leave here. Shouldn't be more than a week. Just a little rest, a little extra cash. I'm just beat. They either act like I'm invisible or a stage prop. 'Here comes the reporter. Set a fire. Shoot something.' Every day feels like you're living in some Gothic novel."

"Poor baby." The white bird was now standing in the middle of her kitchen, alternately eyeing her and the appliances. It ruffled its feathers, as if settling in. Snow flicked off its body and floated to the floor to melt in little pools.

"Are you OK?" Ted asked again. "Anything wrong?"

"I'm fine. I miss you. I'm afraid the furnace might need work. I wish you could come home." She wasn't even thinking as she said these things, concentrating on the bird. Its head was level with the top of her refrigerator, a bird five feet tall.

"The furnance ought to hold. Winter's almost over. Call Rob if there's a problem. Don't try to fix it yourself. I'll call when I'm ready to leave, I'd say a week to ten days. I should be home by the end of the month. Love you."

Nadia listened to the emptiness of the line, empty space connecting her to South America, to Ted. She replaced the receiver slowly, hoping she wouldn't alarm the bird. But it seemed perfectly calm, curious about her kitchen. The back door stood open and a small mound of snow was forming on the doorsill. Nadia decided to close the door, but didn't know if she wanted the bird in or out.

"That call came from some island in the Caribbean, near Venezuela, several thousands of miles away," she told the bird. "My husband says the furnace ought to hold. Last time he told me the snow tires needed checking. How would he know?"

She gave a little bitter laugh. "Ted's notion of home is a hotel room. He probably has to look up the address every time he comes back here."

From the corner of her eye she spotted Cody creeping around the legs of the table, his fur fluffed, his eyes slitted at the giant bird. Cody hissed, spat. The bird turned its bright eye on the cat, opened its beak, and made a sharp, fast sound like "Crook!" It spread its wings until they touched the sink and the stove, and took a ticking step toward Cody, menacing.

In the five years Cody had lived with Nadia and Ted he'd never been known for his courage. Spitting at the bird one more time, he huddled back into himself and disappeared under the table. In a moment both Nadia and the bird heard him scurry down the hall, his feet clattering like the hooves of a team of tiny horses.

Nadia eased around the bird and closed the back door. The bird looked at her, then resumed eyeing the rest of the kitchen. On the table was a bowl of fruit. The white bird settled its feathers and stretched its black-and-white neck to pluck out a grape, which it tossed into the air, caught, swallowed. Nadia thought she could almost see the tiny grape sliding down the long neck.

Everything made sense now except the fact the bird didn't seem to be afraid of her. A blinding, raging snowstorm was going on outside and this bird was lost and needed food and shelter. The bird continued eating grapes, with a little toss into the air before catching and swallowing each one, a flash of the warty red skullcap. Nadia moved carefully around the bird and went to the refrigerator. She'd never owned a pet bird and knew nothing about what to feed this giant, but obviously it was hungry and it would know what it liked to eat.

She removed items at random. Lettuce, last night's leftover steak, an apple, cheese, mushrooms, carrots, lunchmeat, bread, tomatoes, cottage cheese, devil's food cake. She cut everything into small pieces and placed them on the table near the grapes. She filled a casserole dish with water then opened a can of Cody's cat food and offered a bowl of Cody's kibble. From the cupboard she took cans of chopped clams, olives, minestrone soup, opened them, and set them down. She got out sunflower seeds and cereal. The bird went for the clams right away, drinking up the juice with a little kissing sound.

The bill, as long as a conductor's baton, opened and closed like a pair of scissors. The tongue was a long blue worm that shot out from between the bill, the same blue as deeply frozen ice. She wondered where its ears were, hidden beneath the pin feathers. While she watched the bird eat she was tempted to touch it, to feel the feathers. Tentatively she reached out a hand and placed it at the base of the long neck. The bird continued eating and beneath the cold, wet feathers Nadia could feel the heat and energy of its body.

Such a beautiful bird. With its wings tucked back the black wingtips rested together like a feathered bustle that moved slightly with every mouthful. It paid no attention to her, as if it might be used to people.

Nadia left the bird eating from the top of her kitchen table and went into the bedroom to dress. Cody was curled up watchfully on the pillows, his green eyes bright and staring. "Some cat you are," she said to Cody. "Cats are supposed to catch birds." And she laughed at the idea of Cody, one-tenth this bird's size, catching or even threatening it.

Pulling on a heavy sweater and jeans she decided it wouldn't hurt to let the bird stay in the house until the worst of the storm was over. Certainly, if it wanted to leave it would show some agitation, and she would simply open the back door. She wondered how many of her neighbors had seen this big fellow, if he'd been striding through the neighborhood all night, all morning, or if he'd been blown in on the winds of the storm and just landed in her backyard.

The black-and-white markings and the red cap on the top of the skull made such a distinctive pattern she was sure she could identify it. It looked like a jester in mime, the way penguins look like small people swimming in tuxedos. She pulled out a field guide and began thumbing the pages. It was definitely a heron or a crane of some kind, but after ruling out egrets and ibises the only thing it really resembled was the whooping crane. But even then the match wasn't right. Whooping cranes are all white except for a black mask. This bird, although the same height and build, sported the red cap and those lovely black markings along the throat and at the tips of the wings, that bustle. Besides, the fifty or so whooping cranes left in the country, according to the field guide, were strung out in a narrow line running from New Orleans up the Mississippi into northern Canada. It seemed quite unlikely even a lost whooping crane would end up as far east as Massachusetts.

Nadia studied the bird as it picked among the pieces of food on the table. She knew nothing about wild animals. As a child Nadia had believed foxes were a cross between dogs and cats, a belief she held as strongly as most children believe in Santa Claus. Years ago her mother had driven her into Pennsylvania hill country to show her what she thought were "albino pheasants." Her mother, an apartment dweller all her life, was quite thrilled with her discovery and did not take kindly to Nadia's assertions that what they were looking at were common snow geese.

She went into the office and booted up the computer. She accessed the data bank at a neighboring college and set about getting information on cranes. By the end of the morning she was quite sure the large bird, which was now inspecting the rest of the house, was a Japanese or Manchurian crane.

"In Japan, the Bird of Happiness is the symbol for eternal

youth and joy, a mystical figure like the unicorn. The Japanese believed cranes could live 1,000 years, like the pines along the shores of the Inland Sea. When the Emperor Hirohito surrendered unconditionally to the Allies in 1945 his announcement became known as 'The Voice of the Crane.' Modern Japanese hang garlands of a thousand paper cranes from temples and shrines, votive offerings for convalescence. In the Hiroshima Peace Park a statue was raised of a young girl reaching toward the sky with a Japanese crane in her hands, as if to set it free.

"The only crane to winter in colder climates, Japanese cranes are monagomous and perform an elaborate courtship ceremony each spring, dancing in the snow. The cranes take turns raising and caring for the young. The traditional Japanese wedding kimono pictures cranes, pines, bamboo, and plums—symbols of good fortune."

Nadia kept scanning the screen and learned cranes eat parsley, cabbage, carrots, corn, buckwheat, tadpoles, frogs, salamanders, mice, and worms. As the storm continued to blow outside and information filled the screen, Nadia still couldn't understand how a Japanese crane ended up in her backyard.

He was a pleasant fellow, or at least she imagined this crane was male since both sexes look alike. He would bow and wave his wings at her whenever she appeared in a room. He arched his long neck back until the red cap almost touched his tail and emitted various purrs and squawks. "Crew-whip!" He was courtly, and seemed to have a sense of fun or humor. In the living room Nadia found him busy with one of Cody's toys, a rolled-up sock that he would pick up with his feet and toss in the air, then jump up to kick it before the sock hit the floor. He looked like a tall white-robed lover dancing in her living room. She wondered if he was hearing some bird music, the temple bells and twanging strings of Japan. The only problem was the trail of droppings, like watery powdered milk, which began appearing on the carpeting and floors in spots the size of half-dollars.

Nadia thought he might have been trained, like a circus bird. He would eat sunflower seeds from her hand, delicately, never nipping her fingers, and give a short bow after taking each seed. When she turned on the faucet he would warble, funny purring noises, and Nadia thought he might be trying to sing. When the phone rang the Japanese crane showed great interest in the ring echoing through the rooms. Nadia remembered a story about chimpanzees escaping from their cage at the zoo. Their leader, a full-grown female, went directly to the phone booth near her cage and picked up the receiver, trying to hear what was inside.

The last entry for cranes was under *Mythology*, and Nadia read the story of the Crane Wife. A poor farmer was chopping wood one day when a white bird fell out of the sky, an arrow through its wing. The farmer removed the arrow and offered the bird rice and water. When night began to fall the bird revived and flew off, circling several times over the farmer's head. The farmer returned to his cottage, only to find the fire built and a beautiful young woman preparing his dinner. He asked her no questions and that night she went to bed with him as a wife.

In the morning she asked him to build her a loom from a Japonica fir. She said she wished to weave him a surprise, but he must not disturb her for seven days and nights. The farmer obeyed and listened to the sighing of her loom through all the long hours.

At the end of seven days she emerged from the small building that housed the loom holding a length of cloth so beautiful it made glittering spots dance before the farmer's eyes. Its softness was astonishing.

She told him to sell the cloth in town, but never ask a price for it. She promised to weave another while he was gone. But when the farmer showed the cloth to the townspeople no one felt worthy to buy it. Finally a samurai offered to lead the farmer to the Emperor.

The Emperor was highly pleased and told the farmer crane-feather cloth was the rarest material in the world. He would not ask how the farmer came upon it but promised to buy any more cloth the farmer might wish to sell. The Emperor gave him a bag of gold coins and the blessing of the gods.

When the farmer returned he was so excited he forgot his promise and rushed into the small building where his wife was weaving. He saw seated at the loom a white crane, its long bill pulling feathers from its breast, its feet working the treadle. Crane-feather cloth spilled out of the loom and the light of magic filled the building.

"I'm sorry," she said, "but I must leave you now that you know my secret. I wanted to thank you for your kindness. There is enough cloth here to make your life comfortable." She walked out of the building, took a few running steps, and flew off, circling higher and higher in the twilight.

Nadia wondered how the farmer lived out the rest of his days. Lonely people cherish passions that can't always be explained, and Nadia was sure the farmer lost his magic after his Crane Wife flew away. She looked at her crane again, stroked her fingers down his long neck.

The phone rang about mid-afternoon, just as the faint light coming through the storm was beginning to die. Federman, offering to drive over and pick up the finished bibliography, to save her the trouble of going out in the weather.

"Oh no," Nadia found herself saying, eyeing the crane as he scratched his bill by rubbing it against a shelf of books, the same movement as sharpening a carving knife. "I'm on my way into town right now. I have to pick up some things." She did not want Federman to see the Japanese crane.

"The roads are pretty treacherous," Federman warned. "I'd be glad to pick up anything you need."

"That's very nice of you, but I'll be OK." She couldn't think of a convincing excuse, short of a prescription. Birth control pills, Valium. One didn't ask strange men to pick up birth control pills for you. Not that she really needed them. "Just give me a little leeway on the time. But I expect I'll be there by five."

She ran her hand along the strong, broad back of her crane, as sturdy as a horse's shoulders, housing the muscles of the wings. Now that she was committed to going into the storm she might as well make an outing of it. What did one need to provide for a five-foot tall crane? How does one care for a symbol of youth and joy and longevity? Cranes are monogamous, what would he do if she went away?

Locking Cody and his kitty box in the bedroom, for his own protection, she quickly scanned the phone book for a couple of addresses. She left the back door open, to hell with the strain on the furnace. Let Ted take care of the furnace. And then she began to shovel out the driveway.

No one about, the air alive with snow, bright bits of mica cutting her breath. Unfortunately she hadn't used the car in two days and a huge drift filled the driveway, blocking the garage door. Ice and snow. Cream-colored snow. Cloud-colored snow. Soapsud-colored snow. Snow and ice in the air, snow and ice on the ground. As she shoveled she could feel the tinge of sweat running down her back underneath the warmth of her parka. Snow emergency. Weather forecasts predicting fatalities. "If you go out tonight, dress for the party once you get there. If your car stops and you're not properly protected the weather department has determined hypothermia will set in within three to five minutes. Watch your pets tonight. Small dogs left out more than ten minutes could freeze to death." Nadia worried she might die in a snow emergency from simple stupidity. A hole in her glove, a boot filled with snow, forgetting her hat. How the Indians settled this country she could never understand.

While she shoveled she watched the back door, wondering if the Japanese crane would leave the house. Perhaps he would hop in the car with her, looking out the windows as she drove through the city. But by the time she was ready to drive off the crane was still inside. Perhaps he was roosting on the couch.

The day was gone, no twilight, darkness at four o'clock. The streetlights flickered, hazy through the thick snowfall. She turned the radio on, loud rock 'n' roll, to keep from feeling lonely, afraid. Federman had been right about the roads. She felt her car was an iceboat gliding over the frozen surface of the street, sloughing and sluicing from one lane to another until she regained control.

After dropping off the bibliography she piloted the car toward the biggest hardware store in the city, one she was sure would be open even today. Once inside, the only customer, she bought six large paint drop cloths. "You've got to do something to keep busy in this weather," she lied to the two clerks, who'd spent most of the day huddled by the heater playing cards.

One of the clerks smiled. "Would you like to look at our paint selection?"

"No thanks. Not now." She gathered up the drop cloths and returned to her car.

The next stop was on the other side of town and Nadia soon noticed the roads were worse over in this section. She found the address, a small house with a snow-blown sign in front: *Live Bait.* An elderly woman bundled in sweaters let her in and stared in wonder when Nadia asked what kind of live bait she sold.

"Worms, of course." The woman hooked an eyelid down to look at Nadia as if no one would ask a question like that.

"Wonderful." Nadia drew herself up to her full height, taller than the old woman. "Do you sell them by the pound?"

"What do you want worms for on a day like this?"

"Ice fishing," Nadia said with some authority. "My husband and I are going ice fishing."

The woman gave her a smile. "Oh yes, Harv and I used to do that, years ago. The worse the weather the better they bite. There's nothing like it for a young couple. Out in the elements, just the two of you with the night and the ice and the wind." The look on the woman's face underwent a subtle transformation, years dropping away from her. "Before the children come, that's a lovely time. Harv and I spent a winter in a cabin in Greenland once. Just the two of us, before the boys were born." She stared dreamily at the snow. "We were only a couple of miles below the Arctic Circle and sometimes when you'd walk on the snow it would boom like a drum. We got all our supplies by ship from Iceland. Our address was Frederik VI Coast." Tracing her fingers across the steamy glass she drew the Roman VI. "I'd do it again tomorrow, if I still had my Harv."

She sold Nadia five boxes of worms, all she had in stock. The white paper boxes were the kind Chinese restaurants use for take-out food.

Her last stop was the grocery store. She would buy more clams, shrimps, parsley, corn, carrots. She debated whether to buy a newspaper. Would anyone advertise losing their Japanese crane? Had he escaped from the zoo, and were citizens asked to be on the lookout for him? Was there a reward on his head?

But would he even be there when she returned? Or

would he walk out the door, the way he walked in, the only crane to winter in cold climates, going from house to house like a dog searching for its master. She decided to skip the newspaper. If the storm let up the boy would deliver one tomorrow. She could wait until then to see if someone was looking for her crane, the Bird of Happiness.

Snow flicked through her headlights like small birds in flight, a thousand cranes rushing toward her. She felt the beat of her heart keeping time with the strokes of their wings. Flocks of snowy cranes, flying in pairs, guiding her to safety. Spots of color glittered before her eyes. Cranes live as long as the pines along the Inland Sea.

The houses dropped away behind the curtain of the dark storm. She wanted to see him dancing in the snow on her front lawn, waving his wings in greeting. He would take a few running steps to meet her, lifting off into the air, soaring and circling over her car. Tonight she would feel the softness of crane-feather cloth, her cheek against the pure white feathers of his breast.

Angels in the Snow

Someone must have slipped the first one under her back door. It said: *Attack Craziness*. Corrie found it lying on the floor on a cold winter morning, wind blowing the snow so the sky looked misted. She might have scooped up the note like any other kind of litter and dumped it in the garbage. But the note was written on Christmas paper and Christmas was several weeks off. *Attack Craziness*. Corrie wondered if this was her first Christmas present, a message brought by the never-ending wind and swept under the back door of her trailer.

She took the note into the living room and sat gingerly on her white wicker couch. The cold wasn't good for wicker, she'd decided. It creaked and cracked. The paint popped off. Several of the struts had snapped. Bob tried to warn her when they loaded the wicker set into the NuMoon trailer down in Anaheim. Wicker furniture in Gillette, Wyoming, he'd said, would be about as useful as her sterling lobster forks.

Corrie glanced out the window to the rolling brown prairie where snow gathered in wind-devils and swirled toward the sky. Beyond an abandoned trailer she could see the huge, chicken-shaped oil drills slowly pecking at the earth, each set to its own rhythm. *Attack craziness*. Attack the whole damn landscape.

She should've known. The sunny streets of Anaheim were just no place for a man like Bob, with his straw cowboy hat, his dogger-heeled boots. Never run off with a man visiting Disneyland. Still, the man had charm. She'd always been a sucker for charm. And there were some things Bob had been right about. He'd been right when he said she wouldn't like Gillette, Wyoming. He was right when he said he wouldn't stay long. If he had said he would be leaving without her, he'd have been right about that too.

The handwriting on the note was exacting and the piece of Christmas paper looked deliberately cut into a perfect square to frame the words *Attack Craziness*. The chances of it blowing under her back door by accident were impossible to figure. If someone slipped her this note in the night, Corrie couldn't guess who. As far as she could tell, in the four months she'd lived in Gillette, Wyoming, she'd met only three people. That was if she didn't count Bob. But Bob was gone now, off to work the pipeline in Alaska. He seemed to have stayed just long enough to leave her in this landlocked town. Corrie put the note aside and continued dressing for work. Just like any other morning she looked at her bankbook. By her figures she would need another $1,200 to get the NuMoon trailer and all her wicker furniture back down to Anaheim. Damned if she would ever take off with another man again. Damned if she would fall for romance. And damned if she would live through another winter in a place where it snowed, or any place that looked like Gillette, Wyoming.

The next morning there was no Christmas paper under her back door. She decided it was the wind after all. But on the third morning she found a piece of pinkish butcher paper with the words: *Fight Guilt*. Again, the paper had been cut to frame the words and the handwriting had a sculpted quality, a steadiness. Maybe Bob was back in town, she thought, staying at that little hotel above the bar he liked so much, the one he

used to take her out to on a Saturday night, as if that was some
kind of a big time. Maybe this was his way of saying he'd come
back. That's a sadness, she thought. Just when I'm used to
him gone, he slips back in. Damn.

A week later she found a piece of old lady's stationery,
the lavender smell gone stale. The whole piece of paper was
there, complete with pale drawing of bluebells in one corner.
It was the same handwriting. This one said:

> *Do 1983 Income Tax*
> *Do 1985 Income Tax*
> *No eggs, no love*
> *Cigarettes, Milk, Toilet paper*
> *tie shoes*
> *Buy Battery Charger*
> *Speak to that Unfriendly Lady*
> *feed guilt*
> *fight fish*
> *Live through Hangover*
> *get up*
> *Speak to that Unfriendly Lady*
> *Lose 30 pounds*
> *Finish Monument*

Corrie noticed that "get up" was crossed out and "Speak
to that Unfriendly Lady" was on the list twice. She wondered
if she might be the Unfriendly Lady. She decided the notes
couldn't be from Bob. It just wasn't his style.

Corrie thought about the notes while she worked on the
books at Universal Ball Bearing Company. It was Friday, pay-
day, and Corrie knew if she was careful she could get her moving money down to only $1,000. When no one was looking
she toyed with the calculator and figured her departure date. If

she kept saving at this rate she could leave Gillette, Wyoming, on February 17, in the dead of winter. Somehow, the date didn't cheer her much. *Fight guilt.*

Looking around the office, she tried to decide who at Universal Ball Bearing might be sending her these notes. Flossie, the other woman who worked on the books, would die before she let her income tax slide for years. Flossie had an affection for numbers and keeping them tidy that was as passionate as sex. George, the salesman, maybe. George said he only worked eleven months of the year and Corrie hadn't been at Universal Ball Bearing long enough to know. She truly hoped she wouldn't be there long enough to find out. George said he took his month's vacation in the Caribbean scuba diving for exotic fish he skewered with his spear gun. That might explain *fight fish*. But George, who was built like a pencil, would disappear if he lost thirty pounds.

That left Mr. McIntyre, the owner. Mr. McIntyre could definitely stand to lose thirty pounds. Could he be a secret drinker, silent and cold to them all because he was hung over? Corrie studied his green leisure suit, the creases around Mr. McIntyre's skinny legs and heavy paunch. Mr. McIntyre wasn't the type to have a monument. And if Corrie was the Unfriendly Lady, Mr. McIntyre could speak to her at any time.

Maybe it was Bob after all. Perhaps Alaska had changed him. Corrie tried to imagine Bob in a parka, dog fur surrounding his face. *Attack craziness.* She would try the Stockman's Bar after work and see if she could spot him or one of his buddies from the oil rigs.

The jukebox wailed as Corrie shook snow from her blonde hair and the collar of her coat. Her eyes teared from the cold and the smoky bar air. She blinked hard a few times and looked around the room. One thing she knew for sure; she must pretend to belong here. Bob taught her that. The quickest way for a woman to get in trouble in a bar was if she looked like she didn't know trouble lived here.

It was crowded on a Friday night, the tables full up with men drinking, a few early couples catching a beer before going out into the night. Corrie walked up to a stool at the bar, near the elbow. To her left, an untidy brunette was arguing with a pop-eyed man. Corrie ordered a beer, Miller, the kind Bob drank. Her eyes searched the bar again, half expecting to spot Bob, certain he was not here. She wondered if snow looked different in Alaska.

The pop-eyed man was saying to the brunette: "Listen here, Formfit. What you know about the law wouldn't fill an empty shot glass."

"Oh yeah?" the woman drawled. "You're so dumb it took your mama 'til you was seven to teach you the difference between sit and shit."

"I don't like mouthy women," the pop-eyed man said evenly.

"And I don't like men whose eyes look like boiled eggs."

A man came out of the bathroom with a beer in his hand and took the empty seat beside Corrie, next to the pop-eyed man and Formfit. "How you lovebirds getting along?" he said to them. He nodded to Corrie and she recognized something familiar in the tilt of his head or the sound of his voice. She noticed his hands were covered with faint, white scars.

"I might just slug him," Formfit said. "Line his eyes up proper."

Corrie wanted to move up a seat or two, away from so much anger in the air. But the bar was crowded, there were no seats. Bob could walk in any second. He would tell her about Alaska, what it was like to drill for oil in the permafrost.

"It's ignorant people like old Formfit Rodgers here that

makes the American legal profession necessary," Pop-eyes said. His voice was too perfect, Corrie decided, like a drunk pretending to be sober.

"You call me Formfit again and I will slug you."

"You see." The man with the scarred hands turned to speak to Corrie. His hair hung in tight curls to the tips of his ears. "Formfit here is a friend of the accused."

"That's nice." Corrie managed a little smile and went back to studying the Miller can. She couldn't figure out why this man seemed familiar.

"Yes," the man agreed. "I think it is nice. Even a murderer should have some friends. The accused, I mean."

Corrie's eyes widened. "A murderer?"

The pop-eyed man moved between them, facing Corrie. He cleared his throat. "You're interested in this case," he said. His breath was sour like pickles and his voice dropped an octave.

"Not really," Corrie said. "I'm waiting for someone." She wondered if Bob might have been murdered in Alaska, if that's why he hadn't written or called.

"A disinterested party," Pop-eyes said. "That's good. Very good. Now. Answer this truthfully." He paused dramatically, poking a yellowed finger at Corrie. "If you were a white woman, would you like to be shot by an Indian?"

Corrie looked at the pop-eyed man and ran the question through her mind again. "If you were a white woman?" She wondered how being shot by an Indian could be more palatable than being shot on the freeways in Los Angeles. Or eaten by a rogue bear. She touched her blonde hair and looked quizzically at the big man with the scarred hands.

He was laughing, his curls shaking softly. "On a dancefloor. On a Saturday night. She was his wife. But don't worry. Vaughn just wants to know what kind of a woman he's picking up."

Formfit leaned across the bar toward Corrie. "You stay out of this." She pinched her eyes down at the edges. "Vaughn's mine."

"Not no more," Vaughn snapped. "I've got a soft spot for sentimental women and you definitely ain't the type."

Romance, Corrie thought. Love light.

"Slug him for me, Pakka," Formfit said. "Let him have it."

"Bad for my hands," Pakka said.

"Your hands." There was a sneer in Formfit's voice. "Your head." She spotted Vaughn making for the bathroom and hopped off her bar stool to follow him.

Corrie felt Pakka staring at her. The bar seemed suddenly quiet and Corrie decided Bob must have been murdered in Alaska. He would never come walking in here tonight.

Pakka waved the bartender for more beers. "On me," he said. "Those two always make me thirsty and I hate to drink alone. Besides, you got taste. Most women drink Pabst."

"I better go," Corrie said. She didn't want to be around when Formfit and Vaughn came out of the bathroom. She didn't want to talk about Indians who shot their wives. *Attack Craziness. Fight Fish.* The jukebox music thudded against the dark walls.

"We haven't met," Pakka said, "but we're neighbors." He toasted her with his fresh beer and a wink.

"Neighbors," Corrie said and thought of the notes slipped under her back door. From the NuMoon trailer all she could see were the oil drills and a rusted-out, abandoned trailer half-hidden in a junkyard of trash. "Neighbors," she said again.

"Yep." Pakka smiled, his face breaking into light. "I've been meaning to ask you if I could grow beans in your yard."

"Beans in my yard?"

"I read an article about growing eight tons of cucumbers

on less than half an acre. Of course, this country's no good for cucumbers but I thought it might take beans."

"You want to grow beans in my yard. In November." Corrie looked at him closely. This man knows murderers and reads articles on cucumbers.

"My yard's full up," Pakka said.

Corrie couldn't place why he seemed so familiar. He couldn't live in that rusted-out trailer. And he couldn't live in one of those chicken-shaped oil rigs. Still, this was Gillette, Wyoming, and out here the idea of neighborliness might stretch clear to Buffalo or one of the little towns, Recluse or Spotted Horse.

"Pakka," the man said, holding out his hand.

Corrie took it carefully, the way she would handle a loaded gun.

"You're Corrie," Pakka said, as if telling her her own name might free her tongue. "I see you when I'm picking up supplies for the Mona."

"I'm waiting for someone," Corrie said. She couldn't remember his face or his name but she was now sure that this was the man who bought all the broken or unusable nuts, bolts, gears, and pins that Universal Ball Bearing should return to the manufacturer. Corrie had invoiced him a couple of times, $6.00 for a case of cracked heavy-duty washes, $2.50 for a carton of broken chain. "How do you do?" She gave him a weak smile.

Pakka's eyes seemed genuinely pleased. "You wouldn't mind?" He cocked up an eyebrow. "About the beans, I mean."

"Beans?" Corrie said. "Oh, the beans. It might be better to wait until spring." By spring she would be back in Anaheim. She could tell stories about murderers and gardeners.

"Yeah, right," Pakka said. "I'm too busy with the Mona now anyhow."

"Always nice to be busy," Corrie said. "I really should go."

She imagined Bob in a bar in Alaska, maybe an igloo. Heavy parka, his dogger-heeled boots.

Pakka signaled the bartender for two more beers. "I'll walk you home," he said. "After this beer or so. We're neighbors, you know."

"I don't have any neighbors," Corrie said.

"I live in that trailer right up from your mobile home. Of course, it's not much to look at with all the raw materials for the Mona lying around. That's why I can't grow the beans. Too much rust in the ground."

"You live in that trailer?"

"I'll find a better place once the Mona's done. But it's fine for now. Great for my songs. In that old tin trailer I sound like the entire Mormon Tabernacle Choir. I think of my composing in the Dylanesque tradition. Dave Van Ronk. You know."

"No," Corrie said. "I'm a Beach Boys fan myself."

Pakka's face fell from the happy grin and easy manner into what might have been true sadness. Corrie thought his face as fluid as cartoons on TV. Certainly better looking than Vaughn with those popped-out eyes. Pakka had a long, lovely nose, like Bob's.

As suddenly as his face crested, Pakka brightened again. "I'll let you decide if the Beach Boys could write songs like this." He began to sing, his voice strong, imitating a deep Irish brogue.

> *Oh Mamma, why did you steam those Brussel sprouts*
> *With my only suit here in the house?*
> *Oh, those Mashed Potato Blues.*

"Here." The bartender set two shooters of whiskey in front of them. "I should start taking back my beers instead of giving you shots. You keep that caterwauling out of my bar."

"Formfit likes it," Pakka said.

"Formfit ain't here." The bartender turned his back on them.

"I really should be going," Corrie said. She wondered if there would be any other movie but a western on the TV at home. Bob had suggested she learn to knit in Wyoming, maybe take up china painting.

"You just don't have a hair of curiosity, do you?" Pakka watched Corrie put her coat on. He downed both shots before slipping off his stool to hunt up his jacket. "You haven't asked me about the Mona yet."

"Thanks for the beer." But she suspected she couldn't duck him that easily. He would probably walk her home, her neighbor in his tin trailer.

Pakka was at her side as she stepped out of the bar into the snow. "The Mona," he said, "is a synthesis," he had a little trouble getting that word out, "of all Western culture. I'll take you up to the hills some day and show her to you."

"You keep her up in the hills?"

Pakka strolled at Corrie's side. The cold burned her nose and their feet whispered in the hard banks of popcorn snow. "Oh yes," Pakka said. "When she's done she'll be able to look out over 100 square miles. I've given her Da Vinci's smile and the body of an Indian maiden. I'm surprised you don't recognize me, all the time I've spent at UBB. I'm making her out of nuts and bolts. She's going to be twelve feet tall. A synthesis of all Western culture."

"You're making a twelve-foot tall Mona Lisa out of nuts and bolts?"

"There's some scrap iron in her," Pakka said. "Her knees are hubcaps. '68 Mustang with simulated spokes."

Corrie hid her mouth in her mittens to stifle her laughter. Simulated spokes. She cleared her throat and said: "But why here? You could have her looking out over the ocean or something."

"We all came out here looking for the golden west," Pakka said. His voice was somber, as if he truly believed this. "Didn't you?"

"What I mostly found was a handful of dust."

They were at the NuMoon trailer now, snow covering the doorsill. "Thanks for the beer," Corrie said. "Good night." She wondered if she should shake Pakka's hand again.

"Aren't you going to ask me in?"

"No." It wasn't even as if she had to think it over. Pakka was definitely not the type of man a woman invited into her trailer. This man knows murderers, she told herself.

"I'll sing you Italian arias."

"Goodnight," Corrie said.

"On the straight up and up," Pakka said. "Listen, honey. This might be your first affair, you being married and all. But it's definitely my last."

"I'm done with romance," Corrie said. "Goodnight." She opened the door to her trailer and stepped through quickly, closing it fast and throwing the bolt.

"I'll catch hypothermia out here if you don't let me in," Pakka called to her through the closed door. "Then where will you be? Body warmth is the only effective way to counteract hypothermia."

Corrie listened at the door until she heard him walk away in the crusty snow. "You've got no heart, woman," he sang through the moonless night.

Corrie dreamed of waves pounding against the beach, waves slapping irregularly against the rocky jetty. There was the soft suck of the sand as the dying waves washed up the beach. She was warm, the sun shining on her face. Men drifted past her in an endless parade. The waves beat more loudly, someone was shouting, drowning in deep water. "Hey!

Hey!" Someone was surely drowning out there. The voice matched the rhythm of the waves sluicing through the pier. "Hey! Open up!" Corrie struggled through her sleep to reach up, reach through the water.

She opened her eyes. The blankets of the double bed were snuggled around her. Snow hissed against the windows of her trailer. "Hey! Hey! Open up!" Bob, back from Alaska.

She stood at the front door of the trailer fluffing at her hair, the stinging cold of the wind and sharp crystals of snow whirling around her. She saw the streetlights down the road and realized the shouting was at her back door. And that it wasn't Bob.

Pakka stood at the back door. He held a bottle of bourbon and a brown paper bag. He wore a wool cap, long winter underwear, and thermal socks.

"What are you doing?" Corrie watched the snow swirl around the aureole of the porch light. She could see Pakka's sock-footed tracks leading up to her back porch. There were several holes in his thermal underwear.

"I want to come right to the point. I don't want to lay you, you being married and all that." He hiccupped. "I just want some hugs and fishes. I means kisses. Hugs and kisses."

Corrie wanted to laugh at him. Men were as see-through as silk. "You could drown hugging a fish," she said.

He shifted his weight from foot to foot. "It's damn cold out here. If you don't let me in I'll take off this hat," he reached up tentatively and touched the wool cap, "and die of hypothermia. This is your first winter out here. You don't know. You let your head get cold and your mind begins to think you're warm. And then you die. Simple as that. The poor little match girl did it. I'll be dead on your back porch."

Corrie shivered in her nightgown, her nipples hard against the flannel. She braced her foot against the door in case he tried to barge in. "You're so smart," she said. "You'll figure out what a waste of good whiskey that would be." She pointed to the bourbon bottle.

"You can't hide me. I'll be visible by daylight if the snow don't hold. Of course, I won't start to smell 'til spring."

Corrie laughed. "Such drama. You're a regular TV show."

"And wolves," he said. "You don't know. Wolves aren't like dogs. Dogs can't smell in the cold but a wolf can. That's how they find their caches. You'll have me stiff and dead, packs of wolves sniffing 'round your door. You best let me in."

Attack craziness. "I don't think that would be wise." But she wondered what difference it would make. She could close the door, pull the pillow over her head, and even this fool would realize he should go home. Still, she stood by the door. The cold whistled around them. She wondered what color his eyes were.

Pakka sat down on the stoop as if the air had gone out of him. "What's the sense," he said, his voice as dispirited as the moonless night. "It's all the same. Whether you're dying from cold or dying from love, dying from horniness or just plain dying from the holes in your soul. We'll never know if it's worse being a dead hostage or a live survivor. But here." He thrust the paper bag at her, his arm long and white under the porch light. "Someone should finish the Mona. That's all the stuff on the butcher paper. Someone will want to finish her, I know. The rest of the stuff are my lists. Too much TV in the world. We never write to nobody."

He took a long swallow of his bourbon and nestled the bottle in his arms like soothing a child. "Goodnight," he said. Softly, he began to sing a song in Italian.

Corrie watched him singing to his whiskey in the snow on the stoop. Men are like puppies, she thought, demanding to be cuddled, coddled. He seemed unaware of her. Snow settled on the curls of his hair. *Fight guilt.* Leaving the door unlocked, in case he got sensible enough to come in, she took the bag into the living room and curled up on the white wicker couch. She could still hear him, if he walked away or decided to come in. The Italian song was very soft on the night wind.

In the paper bag, as Pakka had explained, were the pinkish butcher sheets full of numbers, sketches, and calculations. There were careful line drawings of what the metal Mona Lisa would look like from various angles. He had designed a wide, firm-footed stance, her arms were outstretched. Corrie thought she might look like a silver snow angel posed against the sky. On a clear day, from a hundred miles away, the Mona might be a flashing mirror of light. Corrie wondered if the Mona would rust.

The other papers were as random as the notes he left her. A few were drafts for letters to a woman named Marilyn, his wife Corrie assumed. She wondered if these letters had been mailed. Bob had neither written nor called since he went to Alaska but it would be consoling to think of Bob's unmailed love letters lying around an igloo near the Arctic Circle.

Some of Pakka's letters were decorated with doodles of a face. Corrie noticed there were never any eyes in the sockets. The letter drafts were lists.

> *Dear Marilyn,*
> 1. *It is not my fault my life is screwed up.*
> 2. *It is not your fault either.*
> 3. *Lynn will not have a normal childhood this way.*
> 4. *Lynn will not have a normal childhood whatever we do.*
> 5. *I did not spend the night with Carol.*
> 6. *You did spend the night with Bruce.*
> 7. *Love without honor is brutal.*

At least, Corrie thought, he didn't shoot his wife on a dance floor. She wondered if he spent his Saturday nights designing his metal Mona Lisa.

The lists, like the one on the old lady stationery, had patterns all their own. Good days were signified by items. *Weld Elbow*, with an exclamation point after the entry was crossed off. Corrie imagined Pakka's bad days as the ones where everything was listed and nothing crossed off.

> *Get Up*
> *Breathe*
> *Brush Teeth*
> *Reorganize Mind*

The handwriting was always steady and sure, as if by marking down each part of his life in a clear hand, Pakka gained some control over his days. Everything weighed equally in his mind. A letter to Marilyn and learning Norwegian took up the same space on his lists. Finding bolts for the Mona's spine and buying roller skates for his daughter sat side by side in the same precise handwriting.

Suddenly Corrie realized the singing had stopped and she hadn't heard him get off the back stoop. She left the scraps of paper and went to the door. The wind slipped through her kitchen and made her dish towels flutter.

He was asleep in the snow leaning against the NuMoon trailer, the bottle of bourbon still cuddled in his arms. She saw snowflakes clinging to his eyelashes, soft mounds of snow curled around his feet. His hands were white as marble with faint grey lines. He looked as lifeless and lopsided as a child's snowman.

"Wake up!" Corrie shouted, grabbing him by the shoulders and shaking him as the snow swirled around them. She felt the snow against her bare feet like tiny knives cutting through soft flesh. "Wake up! I won't stand for you dying on my back porch." She wondered if a person could drown in snow, the little crystals filling the lungs like water. They were all drowning in deep water, she in Wyoming, Bob in Alaska, Pakka in his underwear on her back porch. She shook Pakka again.

"Hello," he said, his eyes bleary with sleep and cold.

"Stand up. Get in here and get warm."

Pakka moved stiffly, shaking out his shoulders and arms, brushing the snow off his chest and thighs. He stood in the kitchen blinking at the overhead light. He scratched his head, pulled on his earlobe. Snow sparkled in the curls of his hair. "You're one cold little lady," he said.

"And you're one silly, noodle-headed fool." She pinched her eyes down like Formfit in the bar. "No romance," she said. "I've sworn off romance. Hugs and fishes, that's all."

Pakka agreed. "Hugs and fishes. To counteract hypothermia."

The Confession of
the Finch

A finch has no true way to prepare for death. Like cats, we treasure nine lifetimes. Death is a secret we must discover while we live. All my gypsies have readied themselves in some way before death and I am like a gypsy vampire, living only through these women's souls. On some mornings, just as the sun rises and the air is pink with the smell of dew, I want to forget I have lived with eight gypsy fortune-tellers. I want to be surprised by death; it is supremely sexual. This gypsy is my ninth fortune-teller. When she dies, I die too.

I would like to die in the traditional manner, listening to sad violins and ringing tambourines. I want the magical chanting, the touching of the jewels and beads. I want the wailing of old men and children at the moment our souls become part of the air. But we will die alone, my last gypsy and I. We have no clan to protect us, no *voivode* to break my gypsy's little fingers, to toss the coins upon her breast. There will be no women to dress her in the five skirts and prepare her for her meeting with *O Deloro*. And worse, perhaps this gypsy will die in her home, upon her bed. If this should happen her soul will be trapped. And mine will too.

I know little of the beliefs my last gypsy has chosen to

call her own. But I know death is more elaborate than life and the mysteries of her new religion will affect us somehow. One of the mysteries is the ritual of confession, as foreign to gypsies as bones in a wooden horse. Because of this, I cannot see my gypsy's thoughts in the confessional. This is the cornerstone of our misunderstanding. As a true believer in *O Deloro*, I have no need for another god. My last gypsy needs both her gods. I am sure this will be our undoing.

This is my attempt to confess her life since no one can know a gypsy more intimately than her finch. This is our plea for mercy.

She has been my saddest gypsy. I don't think she ever learned to laugh and her dreams torment her. I know everything about her life because I chose her long before Natalia died. I was curious about this marked gypsy and knew the moment when my last gypsy fortune-teller was conceived in the Portuguese village of Ponte de Sor. She spent her gestation upon waters. My gypsies are people of the land, the deserts. For a gypsy to lose sight of land is an omen of death. But this gypsy began to bloom first on the river Soraia to the port of Lisbon, then on the freighter across the stormy Atlantic to New Orleans. The soul of a gypsy who quickens on the water can be gifted with a unique sight.

As a dark-eyed child she prowled the levees of New Orleans, watching boats ply back and forth with a look in her eyes as if she might know her own future, as gypsies never can. When she was eight her mother ordered the left eyetooth removed and replaced with a gold one, a tiny ruby set in the middle. "You will always be rich," her mother told her. "And if we are ever parted I will be able to find you by your smile." It was the curse of the long days upon the ocean. Gypsies should never be separated. The power of their magic is strongest when bound to a clan.

I could not go to her, could not save her, until Natalia

died because finches can fly only from death to life. When she, my last gypsy fortune-teller, was placed in a Catholic orphanage and her parents and their caravan moved on, I could not help her. I could only watch as this first mistake, this sin against our tradition, fell upon her shoulders. Her parents wished to be Americans, not gypsies, and that desire cursed us all.

My last gypsy fortune-teller remained in that orphanage three years and during this time her soul became a cinder. The gift of blooming upon waters was lost to her and replaced with a small gold cross. I watched with the eye of my heart as her magic and power drained out of her as the soul of a dying man seeps from his left foot.

She does not remember the day I found her flying on the white wings of another gypsy's death, the music of the funeral still lingering in my ears. But she recognized me for the sign that I am and we left the orphanage, although she refused to surrender the small gold cross. She believed I would lead her to her parents, although they had long been dead. Her father, a bearleader, and her mother, a silversmith, died shortly after they took factory jobs in Chicago. They said they were Armenians, unskilled workers. To deny you are gypsy brings certain death. They did not believe a European curse would find them in Chicago.

My last gypsy fortune-teller still dreams of her parents and often touches the tiny ruby in her tooth as a talisman. The image of her parents is as pure as on the day they left her. High young color, the firm cheekbones. She refuses to let them age in her mind, to allow them the gray that lines her own hair or the dimness of her cataract eyes. My gypsy fortune-teller imagines her mother asking strange women to smile.

She is the only gypsy fortune-teller I have known as a child. Her flower is the orange Aureus crocus, the symbol of the springtime of her soul, just as Natalia's flower was the white Calla lily since I did not fly to her until Natalia was in her sixties.

In puberty, not yet to her full height or dimensions, my last gypsy fortune-teller would sleep with men. They believed she could read their dreams. But when she slept with them the men all had the same dream. They dreamed of her child-like body resting in their hands. A small garden grew at her feet, phlox, aster, lupine. She walked the length of their life lines and her feet placed tiny burns upon their palms.

My last gypsy is cursed. Her father abandoned her; she had no *voivode* to arrange for her marriage. She never became pregnant, which is the deepest sadness for gypsy women, a sign she has had carnal commerce with a vampire. And although she has met other gypsy women, they treated her as an outcast. She never fell in love, as three of my other gypsies did. Her heart never stirred when she awaited a man's arrival; she felt nothing when the men left. She stopped sleeping with men when she had to get glasses and at that time began to wear her kerchief tied at the nape of her neck, after the fashion of married women. The glasses she wore only in secret, those plastic-framed lenses I am the only one to have seen. It is not traditional to wear glasses to see the future.

It was in the orphanage where the dreams came upon her, dreams unlike any I have ever seen before. You can know the secret places in the hearts of women when you watch them dream. I have seen the dreams of centuries, watched the truly mystical dreams of fortune-tellers in India and Eastern Europe. This, my last gypsy fortune-teller, dreams of Christ. He talks to her, shaking a bony finger and clutching his robes around him in embarrassment. In her dreams he becomes an old man, then a child, then the child's own father. My last gypsy fortune-teller's only sexual dream is of the Jew who made the nails for Christ's crucifixion.

A finch must honor and protect his gypsy. But she has

betrayed her tradition, and I am afraid for her. My gypsy has lied, three lies that even she does not understand. Gypsies cannot lie for the sake of their immortal souls. And this, my last gypsy, is Catholic. What her Catholic god will do to her for lying, I do not know. But I do know what will happen to a gypsy who tries to deceive *O Deloro*. I know her fate after death. A finch must know many things to be of service to his gypsy.

She told the first lie just after she received her glasses and stopped sleeping with men. I remember this date as the moment our future was sealed. It was a sultry night in August 1967. This boy, as thin in his body as in his spirit, was going to war in the Annamese Cordillera. He wanted his cards read and the cards were clear. The life card was the Three of Wands who stands on the edge of a cliff looking out over a golden bay at the purple sunset. There are three small sailboats on the sea, proceeding to the Land of the Dead. The Three of Wands stands with his back to the reader; two of his wands are behind him and he carries one wand as a staff for his journey. This boy would die. But worse, as his life unfolded before us we could see his soul was as inconsequential as the little floating boats. Born of a loveless marriage, as were both his parents, this boy had only the spark of a soul. There was not enough spirit to give him a good life in these times or to have him reborn. He would die without a mark on his body and leave hardly a ripple in the world. Even his parents would soon forget him. His death would be a failure of spirit.

My gypsy fortune-teller saw his cards as clearly as I did and looked into his eyes and saw how little light they contained. The Nine of Swords, grieving on his sarcophagus, crossed this boy's Three of Wands. Failure. Death. The boy twisted his hands, running his nails across them as if they itched, and we could tell from the hands his faint desire for the life he had not experienced in this world but hoped to find in the cards. Staring directly into the Tarot, my gypsy fortune-teller said: "You will see foreign lands and sleep with women whose language you will not understand." We knew this boy would die a virgin. But as she turned up the final card, which could only be Death, my gypsy said: "This card gives you power at a moment when you will need it most. Through this card you will find unique knowledge, a knowledge that comes to each of us but once in our lives."

"I won't get hurt?" The boy braided his fingers like willow sticks on the ends of his hands.

"No." This was not a lie. But she had given him his fortune as if Death had been reversed, the sign for Change. "After that moment you will be a different person."

Lying, for a gypsy, scars the soul. My gypsy fortune-teller should have given this boy the opportunity to prepare for his journey to the world of the spirit. Instead, she led him to believe he would live. It was a gift to him he could not use. His death now becomes one with my gypsy's, and she will not be able to prepare for her own.

The night this boy died I saw his death near the banks of the Ia Drang river. I watched him sleeping and knew he was not dreaming. When the bomb went off and the sky lit up over his bunker I saw the red cape of the Three of Wands, the thin heart bleeding inside this boy's body. Since he was not dreaming there was nowhere for his spirit to escape. He drew one last breath and the spark of his soul flickered out. But I saw my gypsy's dream: The Jew making the fourth nail that should have been placed in Christ's left foot, the nail that has doomed us to wander. I watched my gypsy touch herself, her hands moving smoothly over her aged body. She dreamed she was a young girl again, men in her bed dreaming the same dream. The Jew forged the fourth nail in the fire and its heat filled my gypsy's body and covered her brow with sweat. The next day she went to confession.

It was over two years before she lied again. It was in the autumn. This boy had presence; I could tell by the roll of his hips when he walked, the pride he carried along his spine. He would be an instrument of the devil, *O Bengh*, the Evil One. There was the faint odor of cordite around him. His eyes folded in on themselves, like an Oriental's. This boy was too proud to accept his place in the universe. He would be reborn, but as some malevolent thing, perhaps a knife with a life of its own.

For a gypsy, to lie to an instrument of *O Bengh* brings grief to the graves of your ancestors. Her parents, long dead although she won't believe me, will be quartered in ever finer pieces, each strip of their bodies divided in half, and in half once again, and again, until my gypsy dies by the knife she has created.

This boy wanted his palm read, and the blind man who sells newspapers across the street could feel the shortness of the life line. He would die by the hands of those close to him, not an accident and never discovered. He would remain unburied until his next life, as a sword or a knife, had revenged itself on my gypsy.

"Will I die?" the boy asked, and I could sense the stiffening along his spine, his pride in his belief he knew the answer.

My gypsy lied. "You will be in power a long time." And then I watched her as she made the sign of the cross from her forehead to her breast. She reached over and crossed the boy also. During that moment, the wind ceased to hum and all the colors vanished from the room.

It was many months later, in the full moon at the end of a fading season when this boy stood in a rocky outcropping near the summit of Chu Mnang Mountain. The moon made the night shine like noontime, and this boy saw his shadow stretched upon the ground. At his feet lay the gnawed bones of a macaque, killed the night before by an oriental tiger. This boy watched the shadows of four men and saw the blue glint of their M-16 rifles pointed at his heart. His last thought was of my gypsy and how she had promised him power and a long life.

That night, in my gypsy's dream, the Jew appeared to her again. In the fire of his forge he honed the first two nails for Christ's palms. From rough iron spikes he beat the hot metal into sheets thin as paper and the colors turned from red to blue, blue to yellow, and the golden yellow finally became silver. With his tongs, the Jew held up the silver sheet of beaten metal and shaved off four thin needles. My gypsy, in her sleep, cried at the sight of the silver, at the perfect round-ness of the needles, their points dripping blood. She shed tears for the delicacy of their elliptical eyes. Seeing her tears, the Jew placed the needles in her hands and scorched each of her palms with the shape of a cross.

The next morning my gypsy discovered the tears of her sleep had clouded her sight. She saw this world as nothing more than shadows. The Jew had taken from her the true colors of this world and given her colors no mortal has seen. She now knows the exact shade of death, the color of music, the tone of the air, and the hue of thoughts.

She spent that whole day kneeling in confession, her mind closed to me who could only know the ache in her knees on the velvet cushion, the stiffness in her hands folded in prayer for long hours. That evening she got drunk, as gypsies seldom do, and told a blonde woman with no soul to never believe gypsy fortune-tellers because they sleep with vam-pires.

It has been six years since she told the last lie. It was in November and she lied to a young man who had a wife and two small babies. This young man is not dead. He neither sees nor speaks, hears or moves. He is kept in a hospital with only his thoughts for companionship. His dreams are shrouded in clouds. It is hard to know how long he will live, but I am afraid when he dies, we will die too.

Since we will die together, I want to experience her, this, my last gypsy fortune-teller. I experienced Lenore, my second gypsy, whose flower was the pink bleeding heart since I came to her when she was a young woman still living in the Carpathian Mountains. Night after night I took each hair of her woman's beard in my beak, my wings beating fine music and clear air between her thighs. I kept my eyes open as my head and glassy wings pulsed through her body. When she would release me, my wings grazed her teeth and I felt her hot breath on my feathers. Like a cat, I could inspect her. My eye leveled with the curvature of her ear; my beak slipped between her toes. I could move beneath the curls of her hair. During long nights together I discovered the thin, liquid space between her heart and her ribs. I saw her soul had the brightness of a perfect emerald and sat slightly to the left of her breastbone.

I have not experienced all my gypsy fortune-tellers. Some were married, some fell in love. When they died they chose to commingle with spirits of their own kind. But I experienced Natalia at the moment of her death. Far above me in the dark channels of Natalia's dying body I saw the violet of her soul as it faded like a gem without light. She died with her mouth open, as if laughing, and I continued my flight to this, my last gypsy fortune-teller. I have never experienced her but I will do so to honor her because in all our years together she has had no one but me.

The third young man wanted both his cards and his palm read, as if one could cancel out or reassure the other. His life card was the pretty Ten of Cups, the sign for repose of the heart. A man and a woman, arms around each other's waists, are waving good-bye to a rainbow of chalices. Their backs are to the reader and nearby their children play without concern. His cross card was the gray Four of Swords, a Knight upon a sarcophagus, his hands folded in prayer. Three swords hang above him beneath a stained glass window framing a woman and child. One sword lies beneath him. Exile. The Hermit's repose.

We watched his life unfold before us, the happiness of his childhood, the good marriage to a gracious wife. It was perfect balance: the idyll of his young life against the hardships of his maturity. His final card was the Seven of Cups, a black-cloaked figure standing with his back to the reader, his arm reaching for strange chalices of vision he will never hold.

The young man's palm revealed his life line broken in eighty-six places, a smooth hand that suddenly becomes painfully discontinuous until the life line disappeared like rain into the earth. This young man was right to have both his cards and his palm read. There was no mistaking his future.

My gypsy lied. "You will live to be eighty-seven," she said. But his life line revealed he would survive eighty-six deaths.

I have tried keeping count because this is my gypsy's third lie. With this lie she has assumed all the pain she tried to spare this boy. If I can count for her, as I am now trying to confess for her, perhaps in some way *O Deloro* will forgive us. Indecision was her sin, playing faith against her heritage, hoping one would counteract the other.

The counting is complicated. He had twelve childhood accidents, eight close brushes with death before this boy stepped on the mine in the Phu Yen province near the village of Tuy Hoa. I wonder if each subsequent operation, eleven, signifies another escape from death or does each time the body falters, the spirit fails, count as one. I am uncertain. This young man could be six beats from death or thirty-five.

My gypsy's punishment has already begun. The night this young man stepped on the mine she dreamed her last dream. It was the Jew again but he neither spoke nor moved. He hung on a cross, crucified by three delicate silver needles. A fourth was placed in his heart. My gypsy did not know whether he was alive or dead, but she removed him from the cross and placed him in her womb. She secured the four silver needles in her heart. She has had no dreams since then, six years. A gypsy who does not dream has no power.

When her soul quickened upon the Portuguese waters I believed she would make special use of her unique sight. I wanted her to become a *phuri dai*, a wise and revered woman respected by her clan. I thought she might have miraculous visions and be worshipped by our people as we worship the Black Virgin. Instead, we will die alone, no tambourines ringing, no violins. If her fingers are not broken we will be trapped in her grave forever.

Finches are gifted with sight only year by year. We see and contain all of the past but our vision into the future is renewed only on the first full moon of each new year. By Christmas my gypsy will be totally blind. Her cataracts are as clouded as cotton patches over her eyes. I pity her, my last gypsy fortune-teller, caught between two worlds without believing in or understanding either of them.

At times I will move papers or dishes so her sightless eyes can guide her hands to familiar places. I keep careful watch on the knives. Before Christmas I will experience her. I will be the last thing she will see. On the full moon I will rise from her mouth. I am afraid we will all be dead by the new year.

The Strength of
Steel

The cities of my childhood are all the same place, as if we lived in them without benefit of geography. In winter, gray snow lies dead upon the ground. In summer, the air shines hazy orange. At night, one section of the sky is bright as daylight, the coke ovens flaring like another sun just below the horizon waiting to rise.

In those days, over thirty years ago, Pittsburgh, Pennsylvania, was the sun of our universe, international headquarters for U.S. Steel. All other cities paled before Pittsburgh. Life in Trenton, Lorain, Gary, Detroit, Cleveland, and Birmingham was unimportant compared to what our lives would be when we moved to Pittsburgh. My father dreamed of working there in the big glass-and-steel main office. He spoke of Pittsburgh as the ultimate prize in an endless contest. "If this job goes well, the next move will lead straight to the Pittsburgh office. Now wouldn't that be something?"

Industry. Work. Labor Day—still his favorite holiday, a day my younger sister Alice and I always dreaded because it signaled enrolling in another new school. On Labor Day we would pile into the car and tour dealers' lots to witness the unveiling of the new models. Edsels, Cutlasses, Darts, Corvairs. We walked through showrooms filled with gleaming steel.

"My first job was with cars," my father told us every Labor Day. "Announcement Day. They'd hire bands to play. Guys would walk around in tuxedos ushering rich people into private showings. There'd be searchlights and decorations and engines mounted on marble blocks. I'd help set it up. There was a car with a clear plastic body so you could see how it worked. One year I worked the helium machine and blew up a thousand balloons."

Steel. While other children learned the histories of their hometowns, Alice and I learned the Eiffel Tower, built for the Exposition of 1889, soars 984 feet into the air, double the height of the Great Pyramid. But the Eiffel Tower doesn't stir my father the way the Empire State Building does. As a boy my father traveled from Queens to Manhattan at least once a week to watch as the Empire State Building rose 102 stories. He was only thirteen but still claims 1931 was the most exciting year of his life. Each week another floor or two appeared above street level, "the tallest building in the world." The year and forty-five days of construction somehow translated itself into thirteen months, one month for each year of my father's age. Watching the Empire State Building gave my father a goal. He thought he could see his future.

My father believes an I-beam is one of man's most beautiful creations. He admires its tensile strength, the amount of stress it can bear. His favorite present for a child is a Slinky, a steel spring wound loosely so it can stretch and wobble like jello and even walk down stairs. Over the years Alice and I received dozens of Slinkys, which we traded away for marbles or kites, or lost each time we moved. One summer we tried to straighten a Slinky, placing large rocks on it in a line all across the backyard. We decided we would remove the rocks when our father announced our next move. By then the Slinky and the rocks were buried under two months of snow.

The first move I remember was to Trenton, New Jersey, in the fall of 1953. Alice, age four, broke out with chicken pox. My father drove off ahead of us, and my mother supervised the movers as they packed up our belongings. Movers leave nothing. They packed ashtrays full of cigarette butts, a drawer full of empty paper bags. I lugged a wicker picnic hamper filled with my collection of china animals, my most valuable treasures, too precious to be trusted to the movers. I brought along a tube of Elmer's glue, just in case anything happened to my china cockers or pandas, or my delicate long-legged deer.

At the train station my mother, in her best suit and high heels, carried Alice, who screamed and clawed at the red, itchy blisters. My mother kept slapping at her hands. People came over to ask if they could help, but my mother circled away, hiding Alice's face. My mother remembers that move as one of her greatest triumphs, managing to get two small girls on the train and into the tiny stateroom before the conductor could spot Alice. We sat in the stateroom all day, eating peanut butter and jelly sandwiches. My mother was afraid we would be thrown off the train in a city where no one knew us, in a city without a U.S. Steel plant.

The hallmark of every steel town is the sky. In the daytime stark white plumes of smoke and steam rise everywhere. Every night looks like Halloween, evil eyes dotting the horizon. In the second grade my first field trip was at night, out to the country, away from the glow of the coke ovens, so we could see stars. None of the kids standing by the yellow school bus believed those spots up there were stars. "They'll have to get a new one soon," Ricky Radke said, pointing to the sky. "The one they have now is full of holes."

"Ricky Radke's wrong," my father said as he tucked me

into bed late that night. "You can't replace the sky. Some things are permanent. They last through time. I'll tell you a story, a famous story about something permanent. It was built 1,500 years ago for King Chandravarman, a steel needle as thick as the trunk of an oak tree pointed at heaven. It's a magic tower, even today. If you stand with your back to the pillar you are in the presence of your wishes and dreams. If you can touch your hands behind your back, your dreams will come true.

"But," my father added, "you must dream the right dream. You must want it with all your heart. Nothing silly. A tower that old, built for a famous king, will only honor serious wishes."

This is still my father's favorite story. Qutab Minar is one spot in the world he would like to visit. But he never explained what it means to have your dreams come true, and we lived on his dreams, the future ahead of us like the horizon. At night when my mother tucked us into bed she told us to be careful of our dreams. The wrong dream can come back to haunt you.

The houses my father rented were often in prefabricated subdivisions thrown up after the war. When Alice was in second grade, this became a problem. She would get off the bus coming home from school at any stop along the line, walk up to the fifth house on the left, and march in. By dinnertime, the mother in that house—or our mother—would discover Alice didn't belong wherever she ended up. This didn't bother Alice. To her, the fifth house on the left looked like our house, had kids like our house, had a mother. It made no difference to Alice if this wasn't her particular home. When the mothers asked Alice where she lived, she would answer, "Pittsburgh."

By the mid-fifties we'd quit keeping our clothes in closets, preferring to leave them hanging in the moving boxes. My mother stopped replacing the broken china and we ate off paper plates. Eventually she refused to hang drapes, simply pulling the blinds at night. We used cardboard boxes filled with broken toys for end tables. The tops collapsed from the weight of the lamps. And our parents never worked in the yard on Saturdays. "Why bother," my mother said. "We won't be around to see anything come up."

"When we get to Pittsburgh, we'll have a house of our own," my father always said. "We'll build one and have everything we want. You want a garden, hell, we'll have an orchard. We can sit around and watch the trees grow."

"I want a horse," Alice said. "And a dog and a cat and birds."

My father smiled, as if he could pull these animals from his pockets. "Sure thing. We'll keep the birds in the kitchen and they'll sing at breakfast."

Alice and I were always the "new kids" in schools that used different readers and math books. School became a full-time proving ground for us. I imagine my parents must have been lonely. There was a black-and-white snapshot of my mother and father dancing in the basement of our house in Lorain, Ohio, famous for its taxi-yellow industrial cranes. I remember that basement as cold and dank, a great place to go in the summer when swarms of sandflies hatched on Lake Erie, but a freezing pit in the winter, except right next to the furnace, which coughed and bubbled in a mysterious way. The furnace is in the background and my parents are the only couple at this party. My mother has on her best dress, taffeta, nipped in tightly at the waist with a plunging neckline. My father wears one of his flannel shirts, his Saturday shirts. They hold each other in a tango pose and smile, dancing in the cellar. Perhaps they used a time-delay shutter so, with no music and no one else around, they could picture themselves at an imaginary party.

When we left Gary, Indiana, in 1957, Alice and I were

determined to take our cat, Bekins, named after our favorite moving company. Bekins was our first pet, since we didn't count the goldfish that lived for a week before floating, belly up, to the top of the bowl. We finally persuaded our father to let us take Bekins in the car. "But you girls are responsible," he told us. "Anything happens, it's not my fault."

After the movers cleaned out our bedroom Alice and I dragged a cardboard dish box up there and cut holes in it and lined it with a living room drape. We filled another box with kitty litter and got a fresh bag of cat chow and a plastic milk jug full of water. We put catnip in everything, the food, the water, the drapery-lined box. When our father called us down from our room, our boxes and bottles in order, Bekins was nowhere in sight.

"You let him out!" we cried at our father.

"You're responsible. I told you that before. I thought Bekins was in your room."

"He's gone! He's gone!"

"Look here," his voice was stern. "We have to air the house for the landlord. The movers have to get in and out with the furniture. Maybe he's in the maple tree. Why don't we go see." His face showed no concern. I went over to look at his hands to see if white lines would appear on his fingernails, a liar's dead giveaway. But I never saw white lines on my father's nails, perfect and square as kernels of corn.

The moving van pulled away and we searched the neighborhood until dark. We knew Bekins couldn't survive without us. When we found him as a stray, he was infected with abscesses. My father took him to the vet, but Alice and I believed we'd saved his life. We played nurse with Bekins for weeks. I kept trying to imagine Toto without Dorothy, Lassie without Timmy. I thought Lassie might get along OK, but Bekins would surely die.

My father herded us into the car. "I've talked to the neighbors. When they find Bekins they'll mail him to us."

During the long ride away from Gary, Indiana, Alice and I steadily lost hope. We didn't know where we were going, how could the neighbors? Who were our neighbors, anyway? How could Bekins survive being mailed? Somewhere near Sandusky, Alice and I got in a fight and threw kitty litter all over the inside of the car.

In the fourth grade, I learned the difference between printing and writing. At first I couldn't understand the significance of the letters, couldn't make my hand connect them properly. But slowly I fashioned those Palmer-method S's and L's and the letters joined up. Printing, and writing. That same year, when we lived in Detroit, I realized something was happening between my parents. There was no blinding flash of insight, just the steady growth of knowledge, like learning to write.

For Christmas my mother ordered an expensive color television set. It arrived in a cardboard box as Alice and I wandered in from school. Unlike the moving boxes, which opened at the top, this box opened like windows to reveal the big screen.

"Look at this," my mother said in a whisper, as if my father might be lurking in the hall. "Watch this." She clicked the knob and "Howdy Doody" came on in garish orange and green.

Alice plopped down cross-legged on the floor. She craned her head from side to side, as if a different angle would straighten out the color. "Will it always look like that?"

"Oh no. But that will be our secret." My mother fiddled with the knobs, turning Buffalo Bob more green, then bleaching him out to black and white, just like we were used to. She twirled the knob the other way and Howdy Doody and Buffalo Bob came up in more realistic colors, but perhaps brighter than they should have been. I stood on one foot, then the other, watching my mother raise the volume, set the colors in hues that would later be called psychedelic. Skin tones were a problem but my mother worked at the knobs until she was satisfied. Colors moved across the screen as smoothly as water. "It's a joke on your father," she told us.

"What's the joke?" I asked.

My mother ran her hand through her hair. A worried look passed through her eyes. She pointed to a chair, "What color is that?"

"Red." We'd had that dingy red chair as long as I could remember.

"Never mind," she said. "You'll see." She twitched and switched all the knobs on the television until the careful balance she'd created was destroyed. "Now you try." She sat in the red chair as Alice took a turn at the controls. In no time she had the kids in the Peanut Gallery tuned to the same too-bright hue.

My mother applauded. She rose from her chair and turned all the knobs again, undoing my sister's handiwork. "Don't tell your father. It would hurt his feelings." The colors were now purple and green, and my mother switched off the set and pulled the shutterlike cardboard back over the screen. "Help me now." She put a lamp on top of the television box to make it look like any other packing box in our living room.

My mother removed the lamp when she presented the television to my father. "Merry Christmas," she said. She tapped her long painted nails against the box.

My father opened the cardboard wings, then looked at my mother. "You know," he said evenly, "we already have a television."

"Not like this. Look." She flipped the knob. "This is special."

My father sat back in the dingy red chair and watched a Christmas cartoon. At first I hoped the purples and greens might be deliberate, for cartoon effect. Then Alice said: "Let me. I know how."

My mother waved her off. "It's your father's present."

After the cartoon there was an Art Linkletter Christmas special. Bing Crosby sang "White Christmas." My father sat through it all, thumbing a magazine, glancing at my mother, who kept her back to him and her eyes on the new television. Alice and I stared at the strange green teeth.

My father never attempted to tune his new television. He's color blind, although I didn't know that then. My mother eventually quit changing it on him, bored with her joke. But my father didn't miss the import of what she'd done.

My mother's birthday is in January and the first Saturday of the new year my father always took Alice and me to a department store to buy something for her birthday. Usually he left us standing in the lingerie department while he bought a sheer nightgown and peignoir set. Alice and I would touch the frothy cloth and look at each other in wonder.

This year my father wanted to show us something special. We drove to a car lot, his favorite in Detroit, the one where we had spent most of Labor Day afternoon inspecting the new models. He walked directly over to a black two-door Thunderbird. He pushed a button and the roof hummed and rolled back into the trunk.

"How do you like it?" He looked pleased, light danced in his eyes. "I'm getting it for your mother for her birthday."

My father kept that car longer than any other he ever owned. He bought himself leather driving gloves and for his birthday my mother gave him a little cap that snapped together at the brim. My mother never drove it. She still can't drive. My father took the Thunderbird to work each day and on business trips to Pittsburgh.

"Your mother's given you the wrong idea," he said one night at dinner. "In Pittsburgh they give the Air Pollution Index every night with the weather. The whole place is very civic-minded. They're really cleaning that city up."

"I'm sure all the women wear white dresses," my mother said. It was one of her pet phrases. No one ever wore white in steel towns. Before she quit caring, my mother would store her white linen table cloths in plastic bags in a drawer, but still the soot would creep in. At night, if you picked up your pillow, there would be a fine layer of soot on the sheet.

"My family lived on a plantation for five generations," my mother once told me. "Even after the slaves were freed, they stayed on working for my grandfather because the plantation was home to them. Your grandmother was brought up by people who knew every inch of that property, every tree, and all the animals. Your grandmother used to be able to tell a bird by its song, even the males from the females."

To tell a bird by its song, impossible. In Cleveland, when I was twelve, I realized each town was filled with Zagorskis and Cordrejauds, names even my teachers couldn't pronounce. Prosk. Zschau. I simplified things. I called all the girls Smith, all the boys Jones. My teachers were YesMam. In October I was suspended for having a bad attitude and fighting on the playground.

The girl was smaller than I was, and she flexed her fingers and curled her lip. "You call me Smith again and I'll tear out all your hair."

"Smith! Smith! Smith!" I yelled until I bit into her fist. I kicked her. I punched her in the chest. I pushed her down. I bloodied her nose.

"It doesn't matter," my mother said. "We'll be moving soon. You can keep up with your school work at home." I began going across town to hang around the docks where the ore ships from Michigan tied up. I felt I could easily slip onto one of those ships, escape across the Great Lakes. I wanted to reach Sault Ste. Marie; the French name intrigued me and I dreamed of the Canadian wilderness with black nights, clean snow, white polar bears. Beautiful stars. But I merely stared at the ships. Beneath all this fantasy was the certain knowledge these ships belonged to U.S. Steel. They could only lead to another steel town. A French name couldn't hide the destiny of Sault Ste. Marie.

I realize now we catalogued those towns by disasters. If things went smoothly the town was forgotten. The only thing I remember about Orange, Texas, is that it smelled of the sea.

By 1963 I was fifteen, Alice fourteen, and we had moved eighteen times. The world felt flexible. Alice and I longed to move to Paris or New Orleans. If steel was the basis of modern economy, the rock heart, as my father said, we logically deduced there must be steel mills in Paris. Instead, we moved to Birmingham, Alabama. New Orleans was only 350 miles to the west, but we never visited there. My parents believed traveling was for people with nothing better to do.

Youngstown, Ohio, 1964. Until then, my family held together like a water bug skating across the surface of a pond, a delicate balance of many parts moving in the same direction. We went to Youngstown because my father believed this would be the penultimate move. This time, if he supervised the job in Youngstown well, he would be rewarded with Pittsburgh.

He was so convinced of this long and steady future, he began plans to build a house. Mortgage payments frightened him, and it scared him to possess anything larger than the Thunderbird, but he wanted to build his dream house, outside his dream city, his own Empire State Building, rising from his own land.

With all these dreams in mind my father decided to economize in Youngstown. He made a big show of it, driving us out to the newer suburbs to walk through a grand place with four bedrooms, a fireplace, and well-tended shrubs beneath the FOR SALE sign. I remember wishing it would rain, great sheets of water washing the sight of that house from my field of vision.

"We'll have a house like this. Very soon." He looked at the property with the wide and hungry eyes of a lover. "We'll build it and have everything we want. Your mother will have a laundry room. You'll each have your own bedroom. Would you girls like that?"

My father was settled into the habit of speaking to Alice and me as if we were still in sixth grade, although I would graduate from high school that year. I still marvel at how blind he was when Alice and I would stay out all night or ask him to pick up Tampax at the store. Time seemed to have stopped for my father. He spoke in the royal "we" as if he were governing a distant country.

When he had announced the move to Youngstown, we begged him to let us stay in Birmingham. I volunteered to live in an orphanage so I could graduate from high school. Alice wanted to live with her girl friend so she could try out for cheerleading. My mother threatened to divorce him. He called the movers, gave notice to the landlord, and told us we would be moving over Christmas.

Our house in Youngstown had a mud yard and snow blew through cracks in the windows and under the front door sill. Every room held the dusty smell of dry rot. We moved right in with our cardboard-box furniture and paper plates. My father spent his spare time in the kitchen, the warmest room in the house, sitting at a cardtable, brooding over scraps of paper filled with figures and architectural promotions showing new brick-and-glass homes.

In Youngstown, I realized Pittsburgh, if we ever got there, would be too late for me.

Alice was never home, staying days on end with her new friends. She began smoking menthol cigarettes and developed a passion for rum-and-cokes. She would climb out the window at night and throw rocks or snowballs at dawn, her signal for me to let her in.

My mother faded away. Since the move to Youngstown, she'd quit polishing her nails. She stopped getting dressed in the mornings and spent her days in her ratty old bathrobe. One afternoon in March, during a snow storm, I came home to find all her nightgowns and peignoires hanging on a line across the yard. The colorful silks snapped in the strong wind, twisting and knotting around each other, a riot of empty colors floating above the dirty snow.

My mother was in her bathrobe and slippers, sweeping snow out the front door. She said nothing to me. She continued sweeping and sweeping, as if she wanted to sweep all the snow and soot in Youngstown away from her forever. An hour later, I came down from the room Alice and I shared and she was still sweeping, letting the cold air in. I sat in the living room, huddled in a blanket, and watched her. Thin trickles of blood from the blisters on her hands ran down the handle of the broom.

I knew I should do something to help her, but I did nothing. When I saw the lights of my father's car swing into the driveway, I ran out the back door, through the tangle of her nightgowns, and kept running and running, trying to get warm.

After that snowstorm my mother spent all her time in bed. I drifted through the house with a penknife, gouging randomly at the walls. Alice would stare at herself in the mirror as if trying to memorize her face. My father poured over his figures and glossy brochures.

The fire broke out about one in the morning on a Tues-· day night in April. The arson squad later decided it was caused by the space heater my father absentmindedly left on in the kitchen near his cardtable. My mother smelled it first and came shrieking into our bedroom, her bathrobe flying like wings behind her. The back of the house was in flames. We ran down the front stairs and stood in the yard. The air smelled of charcoal and plastic.

No one rushed in to save anything. We stood spaced apart on the muddy yard as if we were in an empty movie theater and wanted several rows between each of us. The gas lines exploded in fireworks. Glass shot out of the windows, waterfalls of light raining into the yard. A crack like a sonic boom rang out as the second floor collapsed. There was no wind that night, no stars. Flames shot up the color of molten steel. For the first time since moving to Youngstown, I felt warm.

We never found our cat, our fifth Bekins. I tried to believe he ran away.

We spent the next seven weeks in a hotel, wearing clothes donated by the Red Cross. Alice and I went back to school. My mother quit speaking but we tried not to notice. Each night my father would ask what she would like for dinner, and each night she continued to stare out the window to the trees in the park across the street. Usually he suggested lamb chops, his favorite dish, and Alice or I would go to the take-out place down the block. Alice always brought back chicken. I always ordered the special of the day. My mother smiled when I'd bring back a hot pastrami sandwich.

The week I graduated from high school my father came back to the hotel as bright and cheerful as he always was when announcing another move. "Guess what, kids." He carried a certain set to his grin that made his face soft and vulnerable. When Alice had seen that look in Birmingham, she burst into tears, knowing she would lose her latest friends. I never cried. I never made any friends. Like the flowers my mother never planted, there didn't seem to be any point.

This time my father was to be transferred to Ambridge, Pennsylvania, fifteen miles from Pittsburgh, but not the glass-and-steel office he expected. Still, he was pleased with himself. Any place in Pennsylvania would make up for all we had lost in Youngstown.

My mother stared out the window. In those seven weeks she had watched the cold spring turn to early summer. The trees now wore the bright green of new leaves.

"We're going to get the house," my father said. "We'll live in Ambridge while we build. We'll go down next week and talk to the architect and tell him everything we want." He looked at me, his eyes shining with pride. "You can start Pitt in the fall."

"I didn't apply to Pitt." I could see anger cloud his face. "I never mailed the application." I was afraid he would hit me, but I went on, hoping he might understand. "I applied to Wyoming, Arizona, and the University of California at Santa Cruz."

He looked at me as if I were a total stranger. He blinked his eyes and shook his head. I imagined his mind searching for the steel mill nearest Santa Cruz. My ears began to ring. I thought I might be going deaf until he said: "You'll go to Pitt or you'll go nowhere."

And then, as if the situation were resolved and I had vanished from the room, he turned to Alice. "You'll go to Shadyside Academy. That's a good place for a girl like you." He smiled his cocky grin, convinced she wouldn't betray him as I had.

Alice laughed, holding her arms around her rib cage. "Not this time. I'm never moving again. You can't make me. I'm going to marry Roger. You can't stop us."

"Roger? Who's Roger?"

"Roger's family owns a farm. They haven't moved in two

generations. His grandparents live there too. I'm going to have his baby and live with them."

My father sat back and looked at the three women in that hotel room. He looked at each of us carefully, as if trying to understand how we could all be related. He looked at my mother, who looked back at him now, her eyes bright, and I thought she might start to sing. "None of you understands," he said. "You think it's all just houses, places to live. I'm here to tell you it's not."

He stood and went to the window, staring out onto the park. He turned and looked back at us, his eyes the color of smoke. "I've made decisions involving thousands of lives. I'm not about to be stopped by the three of you."

Recently, my father told me steel manufacturing underwent more development between 1955 and 1970 than in the preceeding 100 years. He explained how our lives revolve around changing technology and industrial necessity. I wonder if Ricky Radke ever moved? Did he finally understand you can't replace the sky?

My father once told me he had wanted to watch his family grow up, yet somehow, in the heart of his home, he missed the whole thing. "I didn't see it properly then," he said. "I wanted to show you girls the country and the people in a way I could only imagine when I was a kid. It never crossed my mind you might want something different than what I tried to give."

In Ambridge, my mother began to talk again. "It was a rough spell," she said. "Bad weather." She polished her nails and got dressed in the mornings. She turned what should have been my room into a nursery for Alice's baby. Her taste in furniture became expensive; she favored heavy pieces difficult to move—mirrored sideboards, king size beds, and glass and chrome end tables that are easily scratched.

At the University of Wyoming the stars come out at night so bright and close you can imagine their warmth in your palm. I could get drunk on the smell of a pine tree. I took up downhill skiing and whitewater rafting. I saw antelope and moose that weren't penned in a zoo. Each spring I'd find fledglings fallen from their nests and fill my cabin with baby ravens and Clark's nutcrackers and red crossbills. But mostly I studied rocks, the heart of the earth. I can spend long hours looking at the Rocky Mountains and imagine them reduced to sand on a beach.

Twenty years have passed since we moved to Youngstown. Twenty Christmases, twenty summers. These days my father's very proud of my job as chief geologist for the Forest Service. He likes to hear stories about metamorphic rock. It thrills him to imagine the furnace at the core of the planet, melting rock and thrusting it to the surface as lava. He'd love to witness a good volcano. He sees the earth as a great machine constantly reforging itself. I try to persuade him to appreciate the powers of erosion. I love the process of rough rock worn smooth by wind and water. Erosion somehow threatens my father. When I mention erosion, he counters with the steel pillar erected in honor of King Chandravarman.

My father tells the story of the dream of the fat man who wanted to be thin. When the fat man lost weight, he was left with no dreams. Moving to Pittsburgh and Alice's baby gave my father a new dream, brought him joy and the family he didn't notice when I was a child. A second chance to get the dream right. Alice's son is now a sophomore at Pitt and plays drums in a rock 'n' roll band. He says he wants to study metallurgy and my father thinks he'll make a great engineer.

Alice recently married and within a few months my

father retired and took my mother fishing in Florida. Not that
he cares for fishing or Florida, but he was new at being retired
and thought that's what a retired man should do. He didn't
like it. The Muzak in the shopping malls was the big band
sound from the forties. It made my father feel old. He's always
had a tin ear for music, but apparently he's developed a sharp
ear for the things that make him happy. He thinks if they have
to play music in shopping malls they should play songs he
remembers Alice singing when she and her baby lived in his
new house. His favorite is "Baby You're A Rich Man Now," and
he hums it as his anthem. The Beatles, to my father, don't
seem as out of date as Guy Lombardo.

When my parents returned from Florida, they put the
house up for sale, with the idea they would buy a Winnebago
and tour the country. They thought a house on wheels would
be just their style. My parents have never seen the Grand
Canyon or the Rocky Mountains since they never visited me
in Wyoming. California, to them, is a foreign country, as dis-
tantly related to the world they know as England.

My father began to say: "I wonder if any of them will hold
a candle to old Chandravarman," referring to the projects he
helped build all across the country. "Do you know there's a
crook in the Verrazano-Narrows Bridge?" He snakes his hands
in a little curve to illustrate. "You build a bridge from both
sides and this one was going to miss, no more likely to meet
than you can kiss your own ear." My father loves to tell this
story, detailing the problems in the construction. But he
claims he's never driven over the Verrazano-Narrows Bridge.
His part of the job was completed, and we moved on, before
the bridge was finished.

My parents talked and planned as they waited for the
house to sell. But my father wanted more money for his
house, his first real home, than the market could bear, so after
Florida, my father made owning a home his full-time job. The

fruit trees needed pruning and the lawn needed landscaping. He put burglar alarms on the windows and doors, smoke alarms in the halls. My mother remodeled the kitchen. They forgot the house was for sale.

Then it sold, quite suddenly, and my parents felt they had nowhere to go. For the first time in their married lives they were free. They could tour famous volcanos, see the steel tower erected in honor of King Chandravarman, the Verrazano-Narrows Bridge. They could live in Paris or Japan. But they aren't really comfortable with the idea of going to a place just to see what's there. They believe traveling doesn't make as much sense as moving. When you move, there's always a destination.

The other day my father called to announce he bought a new house, a condominium, "So I won't have to shovel snow or mow the lawn," my father explained. I could hear the old fire in his voice. The new house is ten minutes closer to Pittsburgh, right near the freeway that leads into the heart of the city.

Sunday's No Name Band

Janeen broke her arm at work, an industrial accident we call it. The men in the kitchen have been discussing Workman's Comp and lawsuits based on negligence. If she receives a windfall they think she should build a recording studio.

Janeen's the bass player in our band. Dana and I are going to give her a bath, her first since the accident on Monday. Dana's a nurse. She's also six months pregnant. She straddles the dirty clothes hamper in the corner of the bathroom, giving orders. I'm to perform the actual bathing and my heart knocks about my chest as I imagine Janeen slipping, the broken arm smacking against the tub tiles.

It's Sunday afternoon, raining like it does out here during the winter. Janeen's bath has become a party, mostly because none of us knows what to do with this Sunday afternoon without her. Usually we practice on Sundays in a storage area behind the shop where Janeen works. Matt, my husband and our rhythm guitar player, invited Dana, our vocalist, and her husband Chris who is our drummer. I invited Frank, our lead guitarist. I like things neat, as formal as classical piano, as precise as sheet music. Everyone's here, instead of in the practice space where we've spent each Sunday for the past eight months.

While Dana and Janeen and I are in the bathroom, Matt fusses over his beans and ham hocks in the kitchen on the other side of the wall. Frank and Chris say they will help him. We've decided to call this a Depression Chic dinner, enjoying the pun, trying to mask our disappointment with laughter.

"We should put the deck chair in the tub," Dana says. "That way she can sit down and you can work around her."

We agree this sounds like a good idea, so I go get the deck chair, but it won't fit. We settle for a stepladder which does. This doesn't leave much room to maneuver and my palms sweat as I place it in the tub.

Dana surveys the stepladder, the space heater for extra warmth. "A piece of cake."

"Then why don't you do it?" I say. "You're the professional here. I haven't even given my dog a bath in about two years." Again, I see Janeen falling, the broken arm smashing like glass.

"I do this for a living. Trust me. You'll do fine." She rubs her belly. "Besides, I'm not sure I'd fit." She eases herself back on the clothes hamper, as round and imperturbable as a Buddha. She laughs, but I see nothing funny here.

Janeen looks apprehensively at the tub. "I think if I keep a grip on my elbow you can get everything but the arm pits." The break is too near the shoulder to cast, held in place with an elastic bandage. I'm afraid when she undresses the arm will dangle like something in a horror movie.

I adjust the space heater, directing the flow of warm air. Dana rises from her seat to help Janeen undress. The doctor put the webbing of bandage around Janeen's waist and over her shoulder, where her guitar strap usually sits. Her bass always reminds me of a black lacquer woman she holds in her arms. She keeps a red pick stuck in the facing like a heart.

Dana and Janeen struggle with her boots. "It was so easy to get into them," she moans. Bending is difficult for Janeen, as it is for Dana with her baby. Janeen looks close to tears. "I never imagined it would be so tough getting them off." She stares at the ceiling, studying it. Perhaps she's in pain. "I can't comb my hair. I can't open a carton of milk."

I could get Janeen's boots off in two seconds, but I let Dana work with them. It's good to see Dana in motion, active. A curious light has come over Dana these days, as if her pregnancy wasn't something she carried with her daily, but a new idea crossing her mind fresh and different each time. She often misses what's said in conversations, her cues in the music when she's supposed to sing. This will be Dana's first baby and her fourth pregnancy. The baby is due the same week Dana turns thirty-six.

"Brushing my teeth takes ten minutes. The toothbrush keeps falling over when I try to put the paste on it."

"We have a patient with all the fingers of his right hand, even his thumb, gone. He says he can do everything but hammer a nail." Dana begins to unfasten the bandage. I watch how her hands work in concert, one guiding the bandage, the other holding the ball.

Janeen's eyes look wild in the corners. "I don't want to make a career of this."

"Industrial accident," Dana says. "A slicing machine. There you go." She surveys Janeen's naked body, appraising her work. She smooths her palms on her stomach again and returns to her seat on the clothes hamper.

I hover around Janeen as she steps over the rim of the tub and eases herself down on the stepladder. "OK?" I ask, although I can see she's fine.

"I want a towel," she says, "to cover my face. I don't want my makeup to run. It took me all morning, one-handed."

I can't imagine taking a shower with makeup on. I never

suspected Janeen wore it. I study her face and see how carefully it's done, the fine peach bloom on her cheeks, the dark lashes. Janeen's always been admired for her fine coloring and intense eyes. It startles me to realize the effect is artificial.

Out in the kitchen, on the other side of the wall, we hear something crash, then the deep laughter of men. We look at each other, the way women do. Men in the kitchen. We know what to expect. "I'm glad it's not my house," Dana says.

"Here comes the water." I reach for the taps. Janeen ducks her face into the towel, her back to the shower nozzle. Stripping out of my clothes, I hand them to Dana, who drops them in a pile at her feet. I step into the shower, right under the stream of hot water. It pumps against the back of my neck, spraying over my shoulders, warm and relaxing. Gently, as if her skull were broken instead of her arm, I begin to massage shampoo into Janeen's hair. The arm is a bright blue bruise and looks contagious, as if it could spread across her back, her scalp. As if I could catch it on my hands.

Janeen can't drive, bathe herself, open a can. I feel her defeat. She won't be able to play for at least two months. I know in her mind the band has already dissolved. Dana and Chris will lose interest with the baby so close. Frank will drift off, much the way he drifted in. Matt and I will find something else to do on Sunday afternoons. All of us are too old for rock 'n' roll bands. We play the blues and rock 'n' roll we grew up with and remember more clearly than lullabies.

What kind of band was it, anyhow? We're a band without a name and none of our own songs. We've never even played a gig. We settled into our lives with only Sundays to spare for music, a few hours when we can remember a time when we all felt young and bright and full of promise. A two-month hiatus will be as physical as the break in Janeen's arm.

The shower curtain opens and Dana steps in, on the

other side of Janeen's body. She has a bar of soap and begins to expertly work it around Janeen's breasts. Dana hums, her belly bobbing above Janeen's knees. Janeen sits as still as a fixture while Dana's hands dart among crevices, tucking bits of lather into the curves.

But Dana isn't humming. She's singing, soft and low in that sweet voice of hers, a voice that can stay on pitch. I know right away what it is, as if I picked it up from the rhythm of the water beating on my back.

> *Well, they call it Stormy Monday,*
> *But Tuesday's just as bad.*

I look up across Janeen. Dana's right, of course. I join her, imagining Billie Holiday and her gardenia, the smoky clubs of Harlem. I hear the riffs I would do on the piano and my fingers begin to chord on Janeen's head. The rush of the water makes us sound better than we actually are, adding the beat like Chris's drums and fills. The tile of the tub acts as an echo chamber and the song becomes as thick as the steam rising all around us. "Wednesday's worse, and Thursday's all so sad." We sing from deep in our diaphragms, watching each other's faces so we don't take a breath at the same moment. Janeen straightens. Her face comes out of the towel and she joins us on the next verse.

> *The eagle flies on Friday,*
> *And Saturday I go out to play.*

We are all naked and wet and yet for the first time I can really see us standing before strangers, our instruments ringing with sound, our voices rising with a passion no practice session can provide. We will wear gardenias in our hair, dresses cut to show off our shoulders. I imagine Matt in a tuxedo, Dana with a waist again. Janeen and Frank will resume their affair and smile at each other the way they used to when we first began this band. We will all be dreaming in the dark, and our eyes will meet the light and be blinded with the power of the song.

"Lord, please have mercy on me, please have mercy on me." Janeen swivels her head, back and forth between us, smiling. Water sprays over her face and little runs of makeup trickle down her cheeks like beads of sweat. Janeen sings and sings. I've never seen this smile before. I consider asking if I could wash off her makeup, but I know, as close as we are in the tub right now, we are not close enough for that.

We belt out a rousing finale. "Lord, send my baby back home to me!" And we laugh, giggling like girls in junior high. Dana puts her hands on the small of her back and stretches, her belly ballooning in front of her. Shampoo and soap fleck the tile walls, the shower curtain. Steam swirls around us, creating thermals that disappear some place near the ceiling. You can't keep your eye on them, no matter how hard you try.

Janeen laughs. "I feel better." She runs her good hand across her cheek, wiping at the ruined makeup.

The water begins to turn coolish. It will be cold in another few minutes. "You'll have to stand for the rinse," I say. Immediately I'm sorry I've done this. Janeen's face falls out of the smile. Dana has that distracted look again. But we can't stay in the shower all afternoon, ice water beating on our backs. Yet for a moment, that's what we imagined, that somehow if we stayed here long enough we could all come out healed.

Janeen stands and Dana steps out of the tub. I grab the stepladder and follow, feeling the chill of the air in spite of the space heater. Through the curtain we can watch Janeen turn herself slowly under the shower nozzle, washing off soap, shampoo, her makeup.

I reach into the tub and turn off the faucets. From the other room we hear noise. Men in the kitchen, Matt and Frank and Chris. They're singing. We watch each other's faces, catching the glint of laughter in our eyes, amazed, as if we are the only ones to have the privilege of singing on this Sunday afternoon. Dana takes a towel and covers Janeen, daubing at the water running off her onto the bathroom floor. I open the door and the song is clearer.

> *I can't get no*
> *Satisfaction!*
> *I can't get no*
> *Girl reaction.*

Dana's professional hands dry the injured arm. Our heads bob with the beat, our feet tapping time. We wait until the chorus before we join the song.

> *But I try, and I try, and I try, and I try.*
> *I can't get no (DaDaDum) Satisfaction!*

There's a round of applause from the kitchen. Someone, probably Matt, bangs on a pan. We will eat. Maybe Frank will offer to take Janeen home, the way he used to. Perhaps some day we will play in front of strangers. Maybe there won't be gardenias or tuxedos, but the lights will blind us and the songs will rise.

"Saved again by the Rolling Stones," Janeen says.

Saved again, indeed. We know all the little pieces connecting us to our private pasts. We are learning the moments, like singing in the shower, that will connect us long after Janeen's arm heals, Dana's baby is born.

The steam in the bathroom disappears. One minute you can hold it with your eyes, the next you're staring at empty air. It's the same feeling you have when a song is over, the tune hanging on in your mind.

China across the
Bay

Maria thought of the railroad men and shipyard workers who had called this building their home and imagined them pacing through these tiny rooms during the hours between shifts. She turned her back to the room and watched the sweep of the blue-gray rain. She knew the view: the railroad station butting up against the wharf, the dirty quonset warehouses lying between this old hotel and the noisy shipping yards. They were the patterns she worked with, the trains and ships moving in and out while she sat in this room, her studio, designing posters and flyers, painting in oils. Now she could learn the movements of the yards at night. There would be no reason to drive back across the bridge to San Francisco each night, back to the apartment with Phil on a street lined with palms and eucalyptus. Her studio was now her home.

This afternoon she would go over for the last carload. Her paintings were still on Phil's walls. Her terrarium that had been with them so long she had almost forgotten it was hers still sat on his coffee table. She would leave her key in the kitchen and lock the door behind her. Phil had wanted it that way.

There was a faint green coming through the light and

with the end of the storm Maria should turn back to face her studio, straighten it up somehow. Her drafting table was covered with stacks of underwear and clothes still looped over hangers. A pile of handstitched scrap quilts lay heaped in a corner, the colored patches loud against the white walls. Quilts her mother had collected and given her as a reminder of the few weeks they had just spent together after her father's death. Maria's work was buried. Her paints and papers, canvas, brushes, templates, colorwheels, typebooks, designs, and plans were covered with coats or rumpled sweaters.

She found a towel and washcloth lying near her highbacked drafting stool. Her shampoo was in a box by the radiator, next to one of Phil's flannel shirts. She put it on and the tails reached her knees. Fluffing at her hair, Maria climbed the stairs to the bathtub on the third floor, one of the few fixtures left over from the time when this building was a transient hotel. She'd never used the tub on the third floor but it would probably be clean. The third floor was Krueger's and Krueger was very neat.

Krueger was surprisingly quiet, too, his noise orderly, not like the clanging and piercing whistles of the yards and docks. As she climbed the stairs Maria could hear Krueger at work, an electrical saw ripping through a piece of wood. The final cut made a small screaming sound before the piece fell to the floor. He began to cut another board, beginning with that screaming sound then smoothing out to a hum. Krueger was a cabinetmaker. His sounds were like orchestrated music. Even his voice was musical, a lilt to his phrasing when they met in the hall or had drinks together down at Flannagan's. Once she told him how she felt him humming above her as he worked. He only shrugged, as if she had embarrassed him.

The tub was clean and Maria washed with shampoo because she had no soap. She would make a list of necessities. Soap, toilet paper, toothpaste. The bathroom door opened.

"I'm sorry," Krueger said. "I didn't know you were in here."

Maria crossed her arms over her breasts. Krueger closed the door quickly but stood outside.

"I didn't see anything," he said.

"It's OK. Maybe I should have asked."

"Oh no. This really isn't mine. I've just never seen you take a bath up here before." Maria could hear him shifting his feet outside the door.

"I think I live here now," Maria said.

Krueger paced in the hall. "Why don't you come in and have some coffee when you're done?" Maria heard him walk back to his shop.

With her hair wrapped in a towel, Maria left the bathroom to go downstairs and change. But the door to Krueger's shop was open and he called to her as she tried to slip past. "Cream or sugar?"

Maria fussed with the towel turban and walked in. "Cream," she said.

"It's only instant." Krueger dropped a spoonful of white powder into a steaming cup and handed it to her. "Going to live here," he said with that lilt to his voice that made everything sound vaguely like a question. "Really getting into your work."

Maria held the warm cup in her palms. "I haven't found a new place yet."

Krueger looked at her, then dropped his eyes.

Maria shrugged. "Phil and I split up." Krueger picked at some dirt under his fingernail. "No, really," Maria said. "It's over."

"I lived here for a good long time," Krueger said. "Building's heated. Plenty of hot water for the tub. The Chinese joint on the corner will give you credit. And Flannagan's has a TV." He smiled and pushed back his cap. Maria had never seen Krueger without a cap. She wondered if he might be going bald.

"How long did you live here?" she asked.

"Over a year. When my wife left me. That was in my arty phase. I tried to be a beatnik."

"I don't think I'll be here that long."

"I got a lot of work done," Krueger said. "And bought a lot of black turtlenecks." He smiled again.

"Did they help?"

"No," Krueger said. "Anything I can do?"

"Do you have a pole?"

"A pole?"

"I need somewhere to hang my clothes."

Krueger walked back to the heart of his shop, the entire third floor except for the bathroom. Everything up here was orderly, wood stacked neatly along one wall, the saws gleaming, tools hanging in rows, plans on his drawing boards. He was working on a cabinet with a rolltop, the grooved and tamboured pieces of wood lying neatly to the side like a hand full of fingers. "How about this?" Krueger pushed a metal clothes rack down the center of his shop. The rack rattled and cracked across the old board floor. "One wheel's a little loose. The guy at the Army-Navy was going to throw it away."

"Perfect," Maria said. "I can't work the way things are now."

Krueger carried the rack downstairs. "Christ," he said when she opened her studio door. "What'd you do? Sleep standing up?"

Maria pointed to her sleeping bag crumpled behind her easel. She remembered the sight of the white acoustical tiles in the ceiling when she had first opened her eyes.

"I've got a cot," Krueger said. "It's bad for you sleeping on the floor. Drafty. Make a space and I'll get the cot. It'll keep you off the floor."

Maria had uncovered her drawing board and was placing hangers on the rack when he returned.

"You going to sleep on your table?" he asked. "Plan to draw in your dreams?"

Maria laughed, embarrassed. "I didn't know you had the cot here."

"Never moved it out. Cots come in handy." He shrugged. "Like now." He pointed to the window. "You either got to get a curtain or put your clothes over there. They keep that street-light on all night."

"I know," Maria said. "But last night I was so tired I didn't notice."

"This will do for now." Krueger moved a couple of boxes and set the cot against the far wall. He picked up one of the embroidered pillows from her workbench and grabbed the sleeping bag from behind the easel. He looked pleased with his arrangement and tipped his cap. "Let me know if there's anything else."

Alone in the room Maria felt better, more organized. She wheeled the dress rack around the boxes and imagined walking through lines of clothes, the silks and cottons brushing her skin. She placed the rack in front of the window as Krueger suggested. It blocked the sunlight and made it hard to get to her easel, but it would have to do.

As Maria rounded the corner she looked for Phil's car or a light in the apartment window. But Phil was gone as he had promised. Out of habit, Maria picked up the mail. There was a letter for her from her mother.

Dear Maria,
    I hope you had a pleasant trip back to San Francisco, but mostly I hope that you have given some thought to

returning home. I know we have been over this before but it would simplify both our lives. With your father gone I'm not busy enough. You could live here and still do your work and there would be no bills to pay. Women should not be alone in this world. Parents need their children even more after they are grown.

Bought an Art Deco glass water pitcher today at a rummage sale. There are only five glasses and unfortunately the gold has worn off the rims in places. Even so, I'm sure it is a real find.

Please think about what I've said. Let's not fight, but be reasonable. Let me hear from you soon.

Love,
Mother

The rest of the mail was for Phil. Maria placed it on the kitchen table. There was a vase of fresh-cut garden flowers and a note: 'I've missed you. Call me when you get in tonight. We'll have a late supper. Love C.'

Maria wanted to smash the waterfilled jar or pitch it through the window like a baseball. "You've been away too long," Phil had told her. "I'm in love. With someone else."

C. must have a key. Her handwriting looked like clumps of old spaghetti.

It hadn't been that long. Seven weeks. The two weeks before her father died, the week of the funeral, and the month she spent with her mother. Only the garage sales had kept the peace between them, a mad spending of money that calmed her mother. "These'll be worth something some day," her mother would say, fingering the cracks in a Japanese tea set. "I'm not spending your father's money, I'm investing it."

Seven weeks. Can one fall in love with someone else in seven weeks? Maria felt her teeth might crack. Had it been longer?

Maria searched the closets for clothes she might have missed and knocked some of Phil's shirts down onto his shoes. She went through the bookcase and pulled out volumes that were hers. Novels, biographies of artists, books on design theory and color. C. must be the breathy woman who had called that second afternoon when Maria returned. C. was where Phil spent that night when he said he had a flat tire. Phil had given C. a key. C. was why Maria was living in her studio.

Maria carried an armload of books down to her car and leaned against it to stare up at the corrugated tin roof of the carport. Rain clattered on that roof like trains crossing old tracks. Phil had probably made love to C. listening to the rain while Maria had listened to her mother complain about living so far away.

Back in the apartment Maria wanted to create hollows for Phil. Was the collection of Chinese poetry hers, or Phil's? The Turners had given it to them last Christmas. Should she take the two Kachina dolls? She couldn't break the set up, goddesses of the Sun and the Moon. She would take them both.

She took her pictures off the walls and carried them carefully to her car. Her hands seemed to burn when she lifted her portrait of Phil. It was one of her better ones and Maria knew she would gesso it over, perhaps paint a carwreck on it instead.

Leaving the key on the kitchen table next to C.'s note, Maria slipped the lock on the door when she left. It wasn't until she rounded the corner on the palm-lined street that she remembered the terrarium. C. would probably water it, perhaps cut it up and stick it in a vase. She saw it sitting on the coffee table, light from the window glancing off the glass. Phil's welcoming present. The stoplights ran before her eyes, blurred and burning.

.   .   .

"How's it going?" Krueger asked her a few days later at Flannagan's.

"OK," Maria said. "As soon as I heal."

"Heal?" Krueger laughed. "Some of us never heal."

"I mean moving all that stuff." She pulled up the sleeve of her shirt to show him some pale bruises. "I feel beat to pieces."

"He wouldn't help you move?"

Maria studied her drink. "I managed."

"Well," Krueger said, pushing back his cap. "You going to stay?"

"Apartments in this town are so damn expensive. My mother wants me to come back home."

"Back to the heartland, huh?"

"No way," Maria said. "I just think about it when I'm bored."

"I got a lot of work done up there," Krueger said. "I'd work clear through the night sometimes."

Maria toyed with her drink. "There's this playbill job that gets worse every time I touch it."

Krueger signaled Burt, the bartender, for more drinks. "You can borrow some black turtlenecks if that will help."

"It's the little things," Maria said. "I'm getting damn tired of soaking in my own scummy water. I think each time I take a bath up there I'm getting dirtier." She cocked her new drink at Krueger. "Thanks."

"Yeah." Krueger eased himself onto a stool. He sipped his drink. "Listen," he said at last. "I've got a shower at my place. Next time you want a bath, give me a call and I'll let you use the shower."

Maria swiveled on her bar stool to watch the rain sheet across the window. "Do you think," she asked, "I'd get arrested if I showered in the street? In the rain?"

"Listen." Krueger took the drink out of her hand. "Go upstairs and get some clean clothes. You need that shower today."

"Oh, I'm sorry," Maria said. "I don't mean to be such a bitch."

"Go get some clean clothes."

"Really, I'm OK," Maria said. "But thank you. That's sweet."

Krueger continued to hold her drink and stare at her. Maria tried a little laugh that died in her mouth. "OK," she said. "I'll be right back."

They were soaked by the time they reached Krueger's truck. The rain beat hard against the windshield and slapping wipers. As a child Maria believed rain meant the sky was bleeding. She also believed birds drowned in the rain. Her father once told her birds had hollow bones and she imagined the rain soaking through the feathers, penetrating the thin skin, and sinking the birds with the weight of the water inside their bones. Every time she saw a bird flying in the rain she thought it was very brave, heroic, to risk the flooding of its bones as it flew through the storm seeking shelter. Now she saw pigeons scuttling along the roof line of Krueger's apartment building, flying into the wind and rain to arc and wheel away.

"The bathroom's down there," Krueger told her. "Holler if you need anything." He left her standing next to the door, and sat down on the living room floor.

Maria peered into a small room across from the bathroom and noticed a wine bottle with a peacock feather in it, stuck in a corner. Some woman's gesture, she guessed. Except for the bottle, the room was empty. Down the hall, Krueger's bedroom held a big double bed covered with a ratty-looking Army sleeping bag. The walls were bare, no pictures, not even posters, anywhere. The single mirror in the bathroom steamed over as she showered. Maria reached her hand out through the shower curtain and ran a finger across the glass.

Krueger handed her a drink when she returned to the living room. His presence seemed ghostly in this room, too, hugging the corners. Along one wall was a bookcase filled with manuals on cabinetmaking, books on antique furniture and Japanese joinery. A book with a wood-brown cover lay on the floor, the only thing in the room not filed away. Krueger's stereo and records, all classical music, were arranged along another wall beneath the single window.

They sat on the floor, legs crossed and facing each other, sipping their drinks. "I'm just trying it out," Krueger said, looking at the far wall. "Some friends of mine that got divorced kind of willed me this place. And some of their furniture."

Maria looked around the room. For a furniture-maker, Krueger possessed very little, only a round oak table, a metal folding chair, and the double bed in the bedroom. She had expected cabinets, whole roomfuls of cabinets with slight imperfections only the maker could see.

"I'm just trying it out," Krueger said again.

Thunder cracked outside and Maria started at the sound. "You know," she said, "when I was a kid I'd hide under my bed during storms. Or in a cupboard in the kitchen." If I were still a child, she thought, there'd be damn few places to hide here.

"Some people outgrow their fears," Krueger said. "Others grow into them." He eyed her cautiously, measuring how safe it was to go on. "There was this Sunday morning," he said at last. "It was raining. A soft, soothing rain. It rained all day." Krueger tugged at his cap. "My wife left me that day. Packed and left."

Maria looked away from Krueger and hugged her knees to her chest. She imagined him sitting in an empty room watching the rain. Counting each drop.

Krueger stared out the window at the rain washing down

the pane. "Before that," he said, "on clear days I believed I could see China across the Bay."

Maria wished she could frame some sentence for Krueger that would explain how she knew those moments. Although she could see pictures in her mind of times with Phil, they became the dark blues and deep maroons of his bedspread, the softness of his skin, clear as a baby's. Not words she could form into sentences for Krueger. Maria thought surprise might be ocher yellow. Perhaps it smelled like vanilla. "Sometimes," she said, "are always a surprise."

Maria boiled water in a hot pot for breakfast coffee and took her bath on the third floor before Krueger came in to work. But she found she could not simply sit down at her drafting table as she had before. She needed something between waking up and working. When she lived with Phil she could count on the drive across the Bay Bridge to get her organized. Now she began to walk or take the buses full of perfect strangers. Sometimes she was gone all day.

She visited pet stores, the zoo, the aquarium. At the zoo she discovered the blue-eyed caracals stalking their cages like gigantic Siamese cats. The lithe impalas and gazelles fascinated her with the way the light played off their coats and lyre-shaped horns. Watching the lightly spotted manta rays gliding in endless circles around the perimeters of the aquarium, she waited for them to slip their cream-white bellies up against the glass.

But if she visited a pet store too often she was tempted to buy one of the caged animals. Or one of the store clerks would become friendly and try to sell her a hamster, a mynah bird, a baby cougar.

There was a monkey with a tiny blonde face that Maria could imagine in her studio, sitting distractedly on one of the handmade scrap quilts. She had read an article that said chimpanzees could paint. If Maria watched that monkey with the little blonde face long enough she could imagine him mixing paints. She could see him in her studio, painting at her easel, painting on her walls, the ceiling. He would teach her new yellows and blues. She would walk him through Berkeley like a dog on a leash. A monkey might force her to find an apartment. But Maria couldn't even buy a newspaper and look in the Apartments for Rent column.

"Hello there," the sales clerk said. "Still have your eye on Max, I see. Think you'll take him home today?" The sales clerk smiled.

Awkwardly, Maria backed out of the pet shop, vowing to visit Max, the blonde-faced monkey, only once a week. Perhaps someone would buy him, or she would form an attachment to one of the dolphins at the aquarium. Clearly, she could not keep a dolphin as a pet.

Some days she found herself at Coit Tower, staring out over the Bay. She thought of Krueger and how he imagined seeing China beyond the water. Perhaps he saw the stone shrines or ladies' smooth faces surrounded by their stark, black hair. Perhaps he saw the light in his wife's eyes. Why not, she thought. At least he doesn't want to teach a monkey to paint.

Maria heard music coming from Krueger's studio early one morning while she was taking her bath. The music seemed somber and classical but Maria couldn't be sure because Krueger's hammering and sawing cut through harshly. There was no flow or bending of his work to the music, more like a gun-fire staccato spoiling the sound.

In the hall she stopped to listen, wondering if this was deliberate. Just as a delicate violin solo began, Krueger started to hammer, the beats falling irregularly over the violin notes. There was nothing soothing about this noise and Maria wished he would stop and work in time to the music. The violin solo went on, the notes rising and drifting loudly in the air when Maria realized she was staring into Krueger's eyes, his hammer raised in midswing as he looked out of his studio at her.

"Don't care for Vivaldi?" Krueger asked. He placed his hammer on his workbench and wiped the palms of his hands on the sides of his jeans.

"I bet you can't dance either," Maria said. "You got no sense of rhythm."

"I can dance," Krueger said. He walked across the studio and took Maria in his arms, two-stepping back into the workroom and guiding her around the electric saws and stacks of lumber. Horns had joined the violin and the full orchestra began to play, the percussion section swelling the sound to the ending crescendo. Krueger held Maria tightly, leading her with light-footed glides and swift turns around the unfinished cabinets and tables. A smell of fir or juniper hung in the air like the scent of fine tea.

Krueger danced her quickly through the room as the next selection began, a funeral march, led by a harpsichord. He was not slowed by the music or Maria as she stumbled barefooted along with him.

"You probably don't dance in your sleep," Krueger said. "My wife, she used to claim she danced in her sleep."

"Is that what all this is about?" Maria asked, breathless as he whirled her through the studio. Maria watched their shadows flit across the rectangle of morning sunshine on the floor. "Your wife," she said. "Dancing in the morning."

"You Methodist or something?" Krueger asked. "What's wrong with dancing in the morning?"

Maria silently followed his lead, feeling the sawdust shavings tickling the soles of her feet. She wondered if Krueger's wife had a name.

"Music," Krueger said, "is like the grain in wood. And the grain in wood is its life. A record of its growth."

"I'm no Methodist," Maria said, "but I'm not sure I can handle philosophy this early in the morning."

"Best time," Krueger said. "All your brain cells are rested." He released her and drifted over to his workbench. The cassette continued to play, a lively round with each instrument picking up the melody.

Maria watched his back for a moment. "Is something wrong?" she asked, not sure he would answer. "Are you all right?"

"Sure." Krueger kept his back to her. "Krenov has cats when he works. They lie right on his workbench. I thought I'd try music." He began to sharpen the blade in a wooden plane. "I've ruined three pieces this morning. Krenov says you never cut into the wood until you know the feeling of its shape."

"You been up all night?"

"Couldn't sleep." Krueger turned to look at her. "You fashion a living thing when you work with wood. But today it's just not coming to life." He returned the plane back to its place on the workbench next to a stand of small knives. "See this?" He handed her two pieces of wood joined like parts of a puzzle to form a spoon-shaped handle. "The work is everything," he said. "If it doesn't go well, there's nothing else."

Maria ran her fingers over the handle, feeling the slight roughness, a mismatch in the joint.

Krueger pulled at his earlobe. "Except fishing," he said. "Care to go fishing?"

Maria tried to mimic his tone. "The work is everything," she said. "If I don't design something that doesn't turn to dust in my hands, I'll be fishing for my supper."

Krueger unplugged the cassette and handed it to her.

"Try music," he said. "Try cats." In the same motion he walked her to the door. "Somebody in this building should get something done today."

Alone in her studio Maria placed the cassette on top of a box of paints. The brilliant purples and golds seemed lurid after the deep earth tones and pale whites in Krueger's workshop. Krenov had cats; perhaps Maria should buy Krueger Max the monkey to cheer him up. She began to doodle along the edge of the playbill layout, forming a small warbler with a few light strokes. She imagined the warbler in Krueger's warm wood browns with apricot beige for the breast. She drew branches, then blossoms, apple or quince, and wished that the drawing paper were silk, that this was an oriental fan that would ring like crystal when touched. Feel smooth as skin in her hand. Phil's hand had never blistered; Krueger's hands were calloused and tough. Her own hands were a mirror, tiny maps in her palms with lines leading nowhere.

At Flannagan's in the evenings Maria watched the television on the wall. Burt, the bartender, would change her five-dollar bill into ones and take a dollar for a drink only if someone was watching him. Some nights she bet her stack of five ones on the baseball games, generally losing to Burt because she had never before followed baseball. She was glad when she lost; that way Burt would come out even on the drinks he gave her.

Occasionally a man would sit down next to her and try to strike up conversation. Burt cheated these men outrageously when they bought Maria drinks, winking at her as he did so. She had nothing to say to these men; she didn't seem to be able to follow their line of talk or the jokes they tried to make. Some nights she watched the door with a quiver in the middle of her bones that Phil would come in. But he didn't. The only sign she had from him was his handwriting on a letter from her mother. Her mother's letter asked her to come home. Phil had written "Please Forward" and listed her studio address.

She watched Krueger try to fall in love. It seemed a studied effort on his part, as if romance was possible only between strangers. Women generally drank in twos, Maria noticed, and Krueger would go over to them as if he owned this bar.

"Evening, ladies," Krueger would say as he sat down at their table. "I've asked the bartender to bring you another round of drinks. Haven't seen you in here before."

Krueger's approach was always the same; the response from women was varied. Mostly the women left, thanking Krueger for the drinks but pulling away. Sometimes they would be back in a day or so but Krueger never sat with them again. The women who stayed listened to Krueger talk about Japanese joinery, or the famous cabinetmaker, Krenov, who was born in China and had become a boat builder in Seattle and now designed furniture in Norway. Krueger told the women how to distinguish different types of wood by the grain.

"What's this?" one woman asked, stroking her ringed fingers across the tabletop.

"Plastic," Krueger said. Shortly after that he excused himself and joined Maria and Burt at the bar. Krueger told Maria she had a perfect instinct for baseball. He said she could pick the losing team every time.

It was raining the Saturday night Maria ran home, ran back through the wet streets to her studio. She leaned against the door and watched the water drip off her dress and make puddles on the old oak floor. She was as cold as if she had been kissing a statue. In the harsh light of the overhead bulb the stacks of quilts, boxes of paint, posters and flyers, the cot covered with pillows, the rack of dresses and shirts, all made her feel she was standing in a storage room full of other people's castoffs. No one could possibly live this way.

She took off her clothes and laid them on the radiator. In one of her boxes was a bottle of Grand Marnier, a present for Phil, a celebration surprise saved for when she got home. But Phil had had that flat tire and not come home that night. She sat in her drafting chair and sipped the sweet orangish liqueur. She watched the rain fall on the street below. Her body felt hollow, water slipping down the inside of her spine. It seemed to her she had finally located her pain, somewhere beneath her shoulderblades where Phil's hands would have been when they made love.

When Maria awoke in her chair the next morning the Grand Marnier bottle was empty at her feet. Her hangover felt as if she might have sliced off her earlobes. Or stuck piano wire in her eyes. She got dressed and went downstairs, down the street in the rain, and stood in front of Flannagan's until Burt saw her and let her in.

He opened the door with a little flourish. "And whose party are you at?" Burt asked with a smile. "Is this a party left over from last night, or a stone cold original one for this morning?"

"Yeah." Maria shrugged.

Burt walked her to the bar. "Help yourself," he said. "I've got to stock the cooler."

Krueger sat at the bar, a shot of brown bourbon curled in his hands. "Sunday morning drinkers," he said, "best know how to mix their own."

Maria went behind the bar to mix a Bloody Mary. She poured tomato juice, added salt, pepper, and tabasco, but Krueger stopped her as she reached for the bottle of bourbon.

"Try vodka," he said. "I insist. I don't think I could stomach watching you drink a Bourbon Mary."

She found the vodka under the bar. "You always open this joint on Sunday?" Maria asked.

"How about yourself?"

"Special occasion." Maria took the stool next to him.

Krueger pulled a quarter out of his pocket. "Heads or tails?"

"Heads." Maria was thinking about the knot between her eyes. She ran her hand through her hair.

Krueger flipped the coin and caught it on the back of his hand. It was tails. "I guess I go first," he said.

"At what?"

"Stories. Excuses." He rubbed a callus on his palm. "Sunday morning drinks. Sunday morning stories. You know." He raised his drink to her. "Why you're here."

Maria gave a little laugh. "I never realized it was a ritual before."

"It's a good thing I'm going first," Krueger said. "Mine's pretty boring. You've probably got a lulu."

Krueger stared at his shot a moment, then downed it neat. He walked behind the bar and grabbed the bourbon bottle. "Remember when I told you I was afraid of the rain?"

Maria nodded.

"Well," Krueger said. "It's raining again." He brought the bottle with him and sat down next to her.

"That," Maria said, "isn't boring. That makes less than a hair of sense. Nobody drinks just because it's raining."

"Not all the time," Krueger said. "Just today. Some days. This morning when I woke up I wanted my wife there. Sleeping next to me." Krueger fondled the bottle, then looked up at Maria. "See?" he said. "Not very interesting. How about you?"

Maria began making a water flower, setting the sweating bottom of the glass carefully on the bar. "You see, I had a date last night, a fellow who's with that theater group I did those playbills for." She lifted the glass and set it down tangentially to the first ring. "Since Phil and I split up it's been hard, well, not hard," she moved the glass over, covering half of the circle to begin the second quadrant of the water flower, "more like impossible, to imagine another man. But I said I would go out to dinner with this guy." Maria picked up her drink and sipped it, replacing the glass to continue the pattern. "So we have dinner," she said, "and we were going to go to a movie. But while we were walking down the street we stopped at a light." She moved the glass one turn to the left. "Sometimes," she said, "you can see things that aren't there, or maybe there are shadows of things you want to see. I looked over at this guy and I saw my father for a moment. And then Phil." She moved the glass again. "I just ran across the street the other way. I ran all the way back here." She looked up at Krueger, then moved the glass another turn to the left.

Krueger nodded. "You know," he said, "what this place needs is a big-bosomed nice gray-haired motherly type to stand behind the bar."

"When I was home," Maria said, "I wanted to crawl up in my mother's lap and cry. I wanted to kiss her. I never did."

"This woman can't be a relative," Krueger said. "Best to hire someone."

They drank in silence, listening to the rain pattering on the awning over the door. The gray light of the rain was the color of the ocean. It seemed to Maria to be the exact shade she would paint over Phil's portrait. Perhaps it was the color Krueger saw in his dreams.

"I've got to go," Maria said suddenly. She pushed her drink across the bar.

"Easy," Krueger said.

Back up in her studio Maria looked out the window at the railroad tracks and wished she could hear Krueger at work upstairs. She wanted to hear the hum of all the electric saws, planes, drills, anything Krueger had that would make noise. She wanted to splash paint on her walls, decorate the day with sound and color. The dockyard and railroad station were quiet this morning, as still as a world without wind.

There was a knock at the door, and when Maria opened it she saw Krueger standing there with the half-empty bottle of bourbon. He rocked back on his heels.

"I thought you might like a shower today." He pushed back the bill of his cap.

Maria watched the light in his blue eyes. "Yeah," she said. "OK." She went to the corner where she had piled the quilts. Gathering them in her arms, Maria turned back to Krueger. "Let's go," she said.

They walked past Flannagan's, brushing against each other. The rain beat softly on their shoulders and splattered on the colored quilts.

"It's going to storm," Krueger said.

"No," Maria said. "It's only raining."

Mozart in the
Afternoon

It would be nice to imagine my past as somewhere else, a place where things are done differently. And yet again I find myself imagining white barrens of the Arctic where small animals and birds camouflage themselves in snowy colors. In that cold silence only the clicking of caribou hooves can be heard on the loose wind-swept stones.

Sitting in the sun, my feet propped amidst my ferns and wandering jews, I feel beads of sweat roll slowly down my side, staining my fresh blouse at the waist. My gin and tonic is icy; I press the glass against my wrist, feel the cold slipping through the pulsing veins and arteries of my arm. The Eskimo have fifty-two words for snow. They say you don't know a thing until you can name it. Sliding the frosted glass inside my shirt, between my breasts, I feel the beating of my heart. I have tried to break this habit for over twenty years.

"Pressure points," my mother used to say. "The quickest way to cool the body is to freeze the pressure points."

Liesl, my mother, never told me where she learned about pressure points. Perhaps my grandmother taught her, maybe she learned them during the years she spent in hospitals. Now that I am older I imagine some lover searched out the secret places of Liesl's body. That they explored each other softly on sweaty afternoons.

We always lived in my grandmother's house, a place too large for only the three of us. My mother told stories, as much for herself as for me it seemed. She filled the house with pictures of moths that act like hummingbirds, myths of Trobriand Islanders, details of the mating habits of the aborigines. Since I was eight or so I understood the erotic significance of whales with long ivory tusks like unicorns. It was as if she learned about life from the *National Geographic*.

Hot summer days when my grandmother was gone Liesl and I would go up to my bathroom on the second floor. To have a party, to cool off. I carted our supplies to the seldom-used elevator that ran on a track alongside the stairs while Liesl selected records for the living room phonograph. Lemons, limes, cherries, the tall glasses we kept hidden for just this occasion, an ashtray, cigarettes, vodka, gin, the little cutting board for the fruit, a sharp knife. When everything was ready Liesl would turn on the phonograph as loud as she dared and begin making her way up the long stairs. I drove the creaking elevator slowly, trying to keep just above her, the music growing fainter in the humid air.

Propping her crutches on the first step, Liesl would haul her thin body up by the strength in her arms until her foot hit the stair. Steadying herself, she attacked the next one in the same ungraceful manner. Hot and exhausted, she finally reached the second floor, still humming with the music. When I suggested using her bathroom on the first floor she would laugh at me.

"It wouldn't be the same," she always said. Like the elevator, to her it was a matter of pride.

Brandenberg Concerto, second movement. The allegro

has a hurried expectant air with fanciful violins and occasional horn. From the old wardrobe that sat in the hall we took the lurid silk print kimonos we always wore after the bath. Keyed up to the music we undressed, hiding our regular clothes in the bottom drawer where the kimonos had been. Liesl would lay a kimono over each of the crutches making headless, one-legged Chinese colored people on the floor outside the white tiled bathroom. She always made them look like they were dancing, holding hands on the deep purple rug.

Sitting naked side by side on the edge of the porcelain tub we cut up lemons, limes, and oranges, dropping them into separate fluted glass bowls. While Bach played softly in the afternoon air Liesl made sweet drinks in the tall glasses with fruit and ginger ale. I broke the ice from the metal trays; the frozen steel sticking to my fingers, a faint ripping sound as I pulled my hand away. She always put the gin in last, stirring it slowly with a green plastic stick. I sat on the cool tile floor, swaying in time to the music. The gin burned my throat.

"Caribou," Liesl said, "have hollow hairs." She explained that in winter the hollow hairs keep the caribou warm. In summer the hairs help dissipate the heat.

"Is a dog's hair hollow?" Her explanations were always thorough: the function of blubber for walrus and seal, the metabolism of the Arctic char, build up and expenditure of energy in birds. Always a new set of facts for each party. Always Eskimo, always Arctic. "Think cold if you're hot, happy if you're sad."

The Arctic is a violent place. Volcanoes can create new islands. Glacial hunks of land sometimes drift out to sea. In such cold things end with terrible swiftness.

In early June of 1844 three members of the skerry *Eldey* went ashore ten miles west of Cape Reykjanes, Iceland. There they battered in the heads of two great auks, giant flightless birds expert at swimming and diving, a white oval spot between the bill and eye, light grooves along the beak. In the nest they found a single cracked egg and smashed it among the rocks. The skins of these birds were sold to Christian Hansen in Reykjavik for nine pounds. These were the last two great auks ever sighted.

Toccata in D Minor. Baleful horns building in a crescendo. We began with our wrists. Liesl believed in doing things in the order of their logical importance. Pinioning the ice without the use of our hands, our fingers splayed like dancing clam shells. The hot afternoon sun shone pale through the window. Melting ice dripped down our naked arms, huge drops gathering at our elbows before falling of their own weight to the floor. The ice skidded and slid; our hands and fingers pivoted on the ice and performed tiny arabesques.

The ice had to melt entirely before we could move on. Each pressure point received fresh ice and a small shot of gin. Often I squeezed my ice cube, causing it to melt more quickly. I would suck on limes until my teeth ached.

"Everything is functional for the Eskimo," Liesl told me. "Carving a wooden bird snare appeases the spirits of the wind."

Clasping our hands around our necks we cradled the ice tightly in our elbows until the cold water ran down our arms, the long torsos of our bodies, making a sticky sweet smell rise in the room around us. Over the soft violins and cellos Liesl told me myths and legends of lost Arctic beasts and giants. I asked her if she had ever been there, but she only smiled at me.

In little yellow notebooks I collected facts from the Public Library. Eskimo facts to tell Liesl.

"Do you know lemmings commit suicide?" I asked her.

She smiled. "They're good swimmers. Where there are too many of them, some swim to another place far away."

They say fish cannot discover the water, that an islander is the only one who can find the mainland.

Jesu, Joy of Man's Desiring. Languid violins, a proper minuet tempo. Our bodies would be sticky and cool; Liesl would take a fresh piece of ice for her chest. Her firm breasts made a neat hollow for the ice cube. Thin pianist's hands fanned out across her chest as she let the ice water run slowly down her arms, down her smooth belly to be trapped in a small glittering pool in her navel. Out of habit or impatience, I slid my ice across the thin lumps of my ribs, feeling the tingling sensation pass fleetingly over the tiny nerve endings under my pale skin. Liesl said that was cheating: the object of the game was to hold perfectly still.

Her hands were beautiful. The miniature moon shape of her fine clear nails always made me want to hide my own stubby fingers splayed upon her chest like ten tiny clubs. She sat motionless, listening to the music as she held an ice cube over each of my freckle-looking breasts. Using my palms, I tried to balance the ice on the tips of her warm brown nipples. My fingers traced delicate circles in the downy hairs silhouetted by the slanted afternoon light. Our nipples would rise, pushing the ice into the sensitive hollow of each other's palms. The melting water glittered and slid slowly down the smooth curve of Liesl's soft breasts, leaving little wet trails down her belly, lost in the soft folds of her waist.

Often I asked her if I would ever get real breasts, like hers.

"Some people don't," she replied.

"Who?" All the women I knew had breasts, even my teacher at school.

"Men," she said.

Liesl said everything operated according to a rhythm; we always made a fresh drink when Mozart began. We filled our tall glasses with plenty of fresh fruit, ice, ginger ale, and vodka. Vodka for Mozart, gin for Bach. Liesl explained that vodka was a Russian drink; the Russians were the bravest people in the world.

Sonata in G for violin and piano. Rapid counterpoint of the piano against the fluid violin. Liesl listened until the adente before putting her drink down and handing me an ice cube. She moved her leg over just a little on the side of the tub. Gently, searchingly, I put the ice cube in the secret place up inside her. She would smile, sip her drink as I positioned myself on the wet tile floor. The water would no longer be cool; it was only a damp layer over the tiny concrete fills laid between the white tiles. Softly, numbingly, Liesl put an ice cube up inside me. I was expected to hold absolutely still, squirming silently while Liesl gave us each another shot of vodka, stirring it slowly with the swizzle stick. I tried to tell her how the vodka and ice made me feel hot and cold at the same time, how I felt I was soaring into the soft light of the afternoon yet invisibly anchored to the tile floor by the melting ice.

"It's supposed to," she said.

Lying on the tile floor looking through the afternoon light to the plain white ceiling, I could watch dust motes dance and twirl in time to the soft music. I could see the smoke from Liesl's cigarette curl through the air to lie in little blankets separating the dust. Sometimes they seemed to float up and down, back and forth, gently driven by the force of the music. Inside me the ice cube melted, making me feel I would swell, burst, become no more than those little pieces of dust and smoke.

"When the Eskimo first saw airplanes they were very happy, very relieved," she said. She told me for centuries their shamans had been traveling to the moon to bring back the souls of unborn babies. Now the airplane could take them to the moon. They had learned a shaman's secret; they possessed a powerful charm.

Saltz. Piano concerto No. 21 in C Major. Slowly standing, I could feel the dizzying rush as my whole being seemed to drain out of me, trickling down the inside of my legs, numbing every part of me as if I had dissolved. The ice water slowly slid through the maze of childish hair on my thighs, my legs. Sliding around the bones of my ankles, the water would finally seep into my instep, pooling on the tile floor. Ice water from Liesl's body ran slowly down the side of the white porcelain tub, a small glittering stream that caught the light.

Sonata in F. Rondo. A music-box tune in treble piano. Placing ice cubes behind my knees I squatted by the tub in front of Liesl. Sipping my drink with one hand I slowly rubbed ice over the slick hard stump of what had been Liesl's right leg. The stump was wrinkled a bit, not like the scar hidden on her head beneath the thick auburn hair, but like a picture of skin in an old flawed mirror. It felt leathery and dead. I always wondered where the bone was, the exact point within the leathery stump where the bone had been sawed, cut, broken away from what must have been a long slender leg. Sometimes I would move the ice up until I found the hard knob of her hip bone. But the bone vanished somewhere deep in her thigh.

Only if there are objects can there be a fixed form of this world. Even today I don't know how she lost her leg; my grandmother would never tell me after Liesl died. "If your mother wanted to tell you, she would have." Always the same reply.

Liesl told a different story everytime I asked. Sometimes the leg had been given to a fairy princess who later became my fairy godmother. Once she told me my grandfather cut it off because Liesl had been bad.

For a long time she told me it was because she had been

a baby. My grandmother did not want a baby, she said. When Liesl was being assembled my grandmother became so angry at the fine detail work she threw away Liesl's leg in sheer frustration.

"Don't think I don't love you," Liesl always said. "At least I put you all together right."

But the story I believed was the myth of Paija, a giantess with a single leg springing from her genitals. She is covered with gnarled black hair. In the quiet of that frozen world, Eskimo whisper to their children, tell sacred stories about the spirits that guard their souls. To see Paija is to die. Hunters lost in blizzards sometimes see her. These men are found standing upright in the snow, a picture of her in each dead eye. In the long winter nights Paija stalks the Arctic wastes searching for strayed huntsmen to help her ward off the loneliness. The spirits of their eyes dance in the auroras against the faint horizon. Wives and children weep and moan for the lost ones not even airplanes can return.

Sonata in G for violin and piano. Rapid counterpoint of the piano against the fluid violin. The fresh ice is hard; I balance it on the end of my fingerbones, feel it cut into the chilled flesh of my hand. Softly, Mozart plays in the afternoon sun. The little concrete cracks between the hexagonal tiles catch the melted water in tiny pools. I give myself another shot of vodka, drink of the Russians, the bravest men in the world. I think of my mother and the husband she never had. Run the ice slowly up my legs and listen to the sounds of snowy ptarmidgans soaring over the tundra. Eskimo huddle together in snow houses, wrapped in warm pelts and hides against the silence and cold.

Hearts of a Shark

In the British Museum I have seen the jaws of a thirty-six-and-a-half-foot white shark. This one must be between fifteen to twenty feet long. Angrily, he glides through the frothing swells, the gill net dancing and fluttering in his wake, wrapped and twisted around the dull gray body. I stroke the soft hairs on my arm; they jump up electrically.

Through my feet I sense vibrations, the sput of the diesel engine, men's rubber boots treading the deck. The men's fear seems mechanical and I choose not to watch. I think of my small clapboard house on quiet evenings. In that safe silence I can look out to the dune grass, wavelike in the wind. Beyond my silence tires hiss through rain and snow while I watch the colors of my house change. The hardwood floors going from amber to darkness until I turn on the light beside my chair, create a glowing orange disk on the parallel oak boards. Outside a scrub elm rubs gently against the bathroom window.

Knifing through the water with the precision of an electric arc, the shark heads for the open sea. But the net has him bound. Doubling end on end, he comes back to us, toward the trawler. Fish flip from the gill net, high into the air. Her-

ring, menhaden, scup. Constantly crying for spoils of the
catch, black-backed gulls and ring-bills sweep low over the
froth. Light snow melts into the gray water.

The shark is running for the boat as this motion slows.
Snow hangs in the air like dust. Moving so slowly, he seems
gentle as he turns his grinning teeth up to our steel stern. A
sound like chalk screeching down the steel hull. Shouts I can
see but cannot hear from the men scurrying around me. The
jolt as I fall against the cabin.

I don't hear the voices, only the choppy waves slapping
against the boat, the cries of the gulls. The silence of this
shark as broken water races through his dagger teeth, the steel
net grinding against his sandpaper skin. At least half our
length, the shark tries to swim up under us, his dorsal scraping
the side. I can almost touch him; flecks of paint drift into our
wake. Floats bob and spin around us, carnival color against
the gray water. Dead fish litter the sea. Mullet, haddock, snap-
per.

"The gun!"

He dives but is tied, bound to us by the steel net. While
his caudal cuts across the surface, Georgio runs starboard with
the rifle. Below us, open-mouthed, the shark rises again, laced
with the patterns of the gill net, grinning at us like a friendly
dog. His jaws break the surface as the .30-.30 goes off. Goes
off.

I sense other shark drawing near as water and blood gush
from the holes in his head. Shredded sinews of muscle and
nerve float away in the blood from his hollow eye. Still he
circles us, rising and falling like an eagle or condor, encom-
passing vast spaces swiftly, beautifully fluid.

The gun again, again.

His throat looks soft, velvety behind the knived teeth.
As I stroke my arm, the blonde hairs stand up. Imagine sliding
down the long ample throat. Serrated teeth would gently drive

small rivets along my body, each tooth leaving a little red scratch in my skin. Following the convolutions of my breasts, hips, legs. Striping my body irregularly.

Suddenly I am aware of my foot as it moves in my ankle-bones, my pelvis swaying in my hips. The rasp of his denticled lips scraping at my throat, breast. My skin pulling like soft, stretching candy in his jaws.

He is gone, perhaps escaped. The canvas of the ocean seems to steady itself, dead fish rocking softly on the choppy waves. A ring-bill gull, then another, settle into the carnage, grabbing shreds of fish, tilting them down their gullets ravenously. Ropes, lines, gaff hooks, floaters, sinkers, lie erratically strewn on the deck of the boat. They roll gently with the rhythm of the waves. The men talk, trying to anticipate where he will appear.

The green-gray water boils past his head as his huge white body climbs vertically. He shoots up beside us, hollow-eyes in the snowy air, gray water sheeting from his ancient skin. A shadow above us, standing beside us, patterned by the glinting gill net. Pectoral, pelvic fins flash in the fog and mist. Forever he seems to stand beside us in the foreign airy world. He falls slowly. Georgio fires again, again, and still the shark falls toward us. Over us. Tons of momentum.

I grab for the railing as the huge breaker of mist and sea washes over the deck. The slap of the shark settling again into the waves seems far away. I tighten my eyes against the sharp roil of the water. My body is cold, wet. Salt stings my eyes, my tongue. Things continue to slow, to stop. Again and again I hear the .30-.30. He lies quietly on the water, rolling heavily in the rocky, bloody swell. Georgio fires shell after shell into the shark. Bits of his wish-bone brain, his armored flesh, skip away into the bloody water.

Floaters and sinkers from the gill net stick to him like gaudy decorations. I count back the three rows of triangular splayed teeth. Gulls, gannets, laugh and sing above us, settle on the metaled carcass. Fish bits seem alive on the choppy red waves.

Herrera walks over to Georgio and puts a hand on his shoulder, yelling something that is soundless in the wind. The snow seems heavier now, thicker as it collects on the sloping roof of the cabin, the gleaming metal of the hatch covers. Looking around at the exhausted crew, I begin to hear their sounds again.

Both Pliny the Elder and *Skin Diver* magazine recommend going directly toward an attacking shark. Trying to flee excites them. Normally they are slow swimmers but in a frenzy can match a dolphin's speed, twenty-five to thirty miles per hour.

This one is a male, exactly eighteen feet long. Just eighteen feet of garbage. Almost two tons of brain-shot shark.

"Feed him to your pets," Georgio says, pleading with me. His gold and silver plated teeth flash in a grin.

"Sell him to your distributor," I reply. "Tell him it's fillet of sole." With a hitch of his shoulder Georgio starts to walk away, cursing me in Portuguese.

"Your boss," Herrera says. "He got to pay damages." His black little eyes stare at me angrily, accusing me, as if the shark were my fault. He wants money for a new net. I stare into the green-yellow water; it is an oriental color, littered with debris from the wharf. Bits of wood, beer cans, gray chunks of sea ice, an old float. No designs come to mind but the swirl of the shark's hollow eye. Hawaiian natives send still-born babies to sea in bloody baskets. The immortal shark will save them, baptize them.

The smell of salt is gone. Only a faint odor of diesel drifts in the air. There is no edge, no sharpness to this day.

"We'll cut him up no extra charge," Georgio says, his mustache brushing my ear. His strong hands are on my shoulders, warmly working up my neck. Sometimes I feel he might strangle me. Quietly his large, warm hand might slide up and encircle my neck. Like killing a chicken he might twist out my life and lay me gently on the edge of the dock. A slight breeze or the nudge of a boat and I splash noisily into the bay, unnoticed.

Only rats, roosters, humans, and Siamese fighting fish will kill members of their own species. Sharks will not eat other sharks. They prefer freshly injured prey. Their small chicken-like, wishbone brain records only the scent of blood and vibrations of fear. A shark caught, gutted, thrown back overboard, will sink silently into the sea, gorging on his own entrails. Other sharks leave the area immediately.

Georgio winks at me, the way men do. I wish men were born without eyelids so the whites of their eyes would always be exposed. So they could never disappear the way they do when sleeping or making love.

I feel Georgio smile as his hands worry up and down the front of my slicker. I have to be careful with Georgio; his arms bruise my breasts. Moving away, I look for jet contrails in the splotty snow sky.

"A brand new net. Not even paid for." Georgio starts moving along the sea wall, hands stuffed tightly into his pockets. He kicks a clump of ice; it sails into the still water, making a hollow plop. Large black-backed gulls flap on the cold snowy air. They seem suspended on marionette strings between the wharf and the low scudding clouds. Only their cries imply they are real. Sometimes I think I am listening to a recording, the same sounds over and over again.

"You're cold, Annick." Georgio takes me by the arm toward the cannery.

From the open catwalk above the workroom we look down over Herrera, swearing in Portuguese at his small crew. Dank antique smells of wood and water overhang the sharp smell of salt and fish. Already the remainder of the catch is sorted. A slim pile of sculpin, menhaden, and sea robin for the Institute. Even small piles of cod, whiting, haddock for the distributor. Herrera and his eldest son Manny have begun soldering and winding the ruined net. Paulo and Raphael butcher the shark.

Tiny sparks from the soldering iron glint against the sandpaper skin of the shark, hung from the winch, gutted. Blood pours over the triangular teeth. All that is left of his tiny brain and right eye is a ragged hole. His other eye is fathomless, the eye of the Hawaiian gods. A rotting dog has spilled from his gut. In hip boots, Paulo and Raphael wade through the contents of his massive stomach: soft drink bottles, a brown pelican, squid, fish, a rubber raincoat, a metal deck chair, several yards of one-quarter-inch nylon line, a decomposing orange life preserver. Hanging by his tail, his claspers dangle limply forward, half as tall as Paulo. Three feet of cock.

During Charlemagne's reign a knight in full armor was found in the belly of a shark. The armor was complete, only the head of the knight was missing. Sharks were highly prized then. A knight wasn't fully equipped to fight for the illicit love of his lady until he wrapped his sword handle and the palms of his gloves with sharkskin, to provide a firm grip, even when covered with blood.

Perhaps the shark is immortal. He evolved in the Paleo-zoic and hasn't changed significantly since Mesozoic times, a successful creature for the last 70 million years. The shark has no natural enemies; damaged cells regenerate quickly, even after death. He will eat anything but another shark. My direc-tor at the Research Institute claims that unless a shark meets with an accident he might live forever.

Since the spring of 1958 shark attacks have risen from one every eighteen months to over twenty a year. The govern-ment maintains a small, steady staff of us to find out why. My director at the Institute, however, has no intention of finding out why. He simply loves sharks. As do I.

Sitting on the cot in the office, I watch as Georgio lights the small gas space heater, smoke another cigarette while he makes coffee sweetened with Early Times. Through the dirty window I can see across the snowy wharf. In Palazzio's Bait Shop hangs a potted fuchsia in full bloom. An Arctic tern perches on a piling. Georgio slides the bolt on the door, telling me about the vastness, the freedom of the sea.

"That's what the shark thought," I say.

Georgio laughs. "He was wrong."

Georgio sits beside me and takes a sip of his coffee. "In '64 was the biggest run of mackerel ever," he says. "Ran this rig twenty-four hours a day." It is hard to imagine the big work-room as anything but empty, an abandoned butchershop for fish. Only a few rats remain.

"Built to work eighteen men," Georgio says.

He takes a drag from my cigarette. "Herrera, he never comes up here now." Herrera, I know, will spend all day on his net. Paulo and Raphael, I suppose, will go home to their wives.

"You and Herrera," I say.

.   .   .

Georgio has fish-killing hands, calloused and toughened, slick like the strong bill of a bird, a heron or ibis. They slide over my body, entrapping me.

Simply as detaching petals from daisies, Georgio and I undress. His hands touch my waist. They run up my body. They are warm and smooth as he removes my sweater. Stretching my arms, I give my head a small shake as the cold air hardens my nipples. Raising one leg I trap his hand in the whiteness of my belly. His wet tongue and bristly mustache work up the inside of my thighs, kissing, tickling, nibbling.

Deep in my belly I feel the familiar pressure, the swelling as my hips begin to move. The heel of his hand slips back and forth over the taut ball under my navel. My hips, my backbones, roll against the thin mattress. Cold makes the fine hairs on my breasts stand up. My fingertips stroke them, touching the nipples. Georgio nibbles, licks at my long downy hairs. Gripping my hip bones, his mustache scratching my soft inner thigh, he works his tongue round and round. I feel my bones separating, my muscles opening. Grabbing at the ball of my belly Georgio kneads at me, forcing the small bones of my back into the mattress until I come.

I have always wondered about the way men make love. Long minute after long minute Georgio gives me pleasure. Sometimes he presses my elastic organs deep into the small of my back, crowding the vertebrae. He never really touches me, cannot touch me as he continues nudging again and again into my cervix. Withdrawing slightly, Georgio changes the angle of his penetration until I feel elevated rather than invaded. Lifted high into the air until I feel . . . I have no word for this. Georgio doesn't know. Yet his hands explore me ceaselessly, holding my breasts, my back, twisting me subtly into different internal positions.

I am sweating, my arms begin to ache. The thin mattress and springs press into my shoulders. I open my eyes and look down Georgio's body swaying against and into my own. Raising my legs, I thrust my hips and lock my ankles tightly around his back. Squeezing my thighs around his hard supple waist, I wait for him to come. My heels rub his butt. Finally, grabbing my hair, he clutches and moans as little waves run through us.

The small wooden bathroom next to the office is cold. Beside the scummy toilet lies last week's newspaper. Pictures and stories that are no longer news. With cold water from the bowl I splash away the sticky warmth trickling down my inner thighs, almost to my knees. It is quiet here, the sounds of the dock and workroom are muted and still.

I pick Georgio's black hairs from my sweaty breasts, deposit them in the john. Cold sodden newsprint leaves black streaks on my legs and breasts. The hairs on my body rise in the cold. It is quiet and pleasant as I stroke the soft white hairs, watch them jump back from my fingers, standing and waving like anemones in the sea.

Georgio stands behind me, lifting the naked weight of my breasts; his hardening cock presses into the rump of my jeans. Turning me, he takes my breasts into his mouth, one then the other, sucking, pulling at the nipples.

Reaching over the desk I find the Early Times and take a long burning pull.

"You like it, huh?" Georgio says, taking the bottle from me.

"It's cold," I say.

Georgio laughs, bunching his fist he takes a playful swing

at my belly. "Ram it," he says, landing the punch softly below my navel. "You want me to fill you up."

"It just runs out," I say. Georgio offers me the bottle and I watch two terns fighting over a piece of fish on Palazzio's dock. Faintly I can hear the echo of Rudy's laugh, the bitter laughter of the night he left me. Georgio had remained soft that afternoon he came to my house. Embarrassed, we lay on my bed listening to Charlie Parker, and I fondled Georgio's limp cock and balls. I made clam spaghetti for dinner before he went home to his wife. Later, when I called Rudy, he told me he'd already been there, parked behind Georgio's truck all afternoon.

Laughing, I take another pull on the bottle. Georgio puts his arms around my belly. "You like it when I come in you," he says.

And I laugh again. Perhaps that was the mistake. I feel Georgio's arms becoming stronger, holding me tightly. His hand moves down the inside of my jeans. "You like it," he says again in a different voice.

"You have this trouble with your wife?" I ask. Georgio turns me, forces his tongue into my mouth, plays with me, pulls me close to him. His cock is not hard.

Jerking my mouth away I take another sip from the bottle. "They teach you that at college," Georgio says. "Spend good money," he says, "to learn to come a lot." Georgio tells me his wife is decent. "She comes when I make her."

I slip my hand into Georgio's soft crotch. "Not often," I say.

And the laughter again, Rudy's laugh. He's the man you never had, never will have, Rudy told me. The All-American women grow up and marry. All women but you. A man to pay your bills, put up storm windows, drive you home when you're drunk. A man to give you friends, children, someone to talk to on rainy nights. But you've been too smart for him, too smart for me. You don't want my small life. Or his.

"Cold fish," Georgio says pulling hard on my nipple with his thumb and forefinger.

"Fool," I tell him.

"What fool?" Georgio says. "I will have a fishing boat." And his wife will have children, Rudy said. You will have a job, maybe a kitty to keep you company in your old age.

"Like Herrera," I say lowering my voice and laughing. "You and Herrera, big Portagee fishermen." Georgio's silver-plated teeth reflect the look in his eyes; I have never been able to see into men's eyes. The backs of my ears begin to ache.

I tell Georgio he will be bankrupt. His wife will never have children. This is sad. He will never own a boat. He will work for wages all his debt-strewn days.

A woman needs a man, Rudy told me. They get old early, women do. Their hair loses its luster, their skin begins to dull, crack, sag. Georgio's wife can get ugly, fat. He will never leave her, the mother of his children. I would have never left you, Rudy said.

"Maybe when you die they will put the names of your famous papers on your tombstone," Georgio says.

"Better than some carping, whipped wife," I say. "A woman who buys toy china animals, magazines about movie stars. I see your wife in stores, the dull look in her eyes, her hair in rollers as she stares at pictures in cheap magazines." I tell Georgio he cannot make a woman happy.

Fool, Rudy said.

Georgio's fist drifts toward me as I watch. There is a scar on one knuckle where the hair refused to grow.

I am screaming; Rudy laughs. My hands are small and white, small against Georgio's face. I seem to move slowly, grabbing at the flesh, the hair. My blue-covered legs are sometimes in view, my feet pasted on, not part of those blue legs. Georgio's face is soft, rubbery, a doll's face with glass eyes. I want to shatter those eyes. My fingernails fill with hair, skin, blood.

My hand is heavy. Georgio's eyes become clearer, luminous. Rudy's silent laughter fills my ears until I become dizzy. I would like to sit down, to sleep for awhile. I do not know why we are doing this.

Below me there are sounds. I think whore. I think bitch. I think curling bitch. But those are not the words. I do not understand the words.

It is cold. My face is wet, stuck to itself. The teeth in my mouth seem somehow loose. Standing, one hand levered on the cot, a fulcrum, I plant my feet firmly on the floor. The air smells of fish, salt. A cold gray sunshine patterns the wooden floor, over coffee in cups, boots, clothing. My hair sticks to my face. My toes curl up against the cold.

The bones of my hips are against the railing, beside my hands. Small, splotted, colored hands. The hairs on my arms stand up. My breasts are bare and freckled, splattered with blood.

Below me in the workroom Georgio smashes his fist into the mouth of the shark. Bright new blood pours over those denticled lips. Georgio's bare brown arm is streaked, slashed. His bones lie under his skin. My eyelashes rest on my cheekbones and it is silent. Georgio stands shooting the shark and the report is soundless. Snow hangs in the air like dust over the ocean. I open my eyes and Georgio's fist strikes again and again into the slicing toothed jaw of the shark. Blood spangles his arm, dripping slowly into the fish guts on the floor. But the laughter, the strong silent laughter that encloses all this continues. Rudy's face floats away before me as his laughter dies into stillness. I do not know why we are doing this.